Praise for Garrett Leigh

"Emotional and brilliant..."

ALL ABOUT ROMANCE

"Tastefully erotic ... more smart than smutty..."

PUBLISHERS WEEKLY

"Powerful and compelling..."

FOREWORD REVIEWS

"An unforgettable voice in every book Leigh writes..." USA
TODAY

Christmas On Stardust Lane

GARRETT LEIGH

For the people who make every Christmas sparkle for me <3

Playlist

- Last Christmas - *Wham!*
- Darkest Hour - *Low Roar*
- Noël de la Rue - *Édith Piaf*
- Merry Christmas Everybody - *Slade*
- Do They Know It's Christmas - *Band Aid*
- Fairytale Of New York - *The Pogues, Kirsty MacColl*
- I Wanna Be Your Lover - *Prince*
- Winter Wonderland - *Bing Crosby*
- Noël A Pàris - *Charles Avnavour*

Listen on SPOTIFY

Content Warnings

PTSD, addiction (secondary character), death (Bhodi is a
critical care nurse) accident, injury

One

TAM

I can count on one hand the things in life that make me truly irritable. Multi-coloured Christmas lights score high. My brother bending my ear about shit I've already said *no* to a thousand goddamn times is top of the fucking list.

"You need a lodger." His voice booms through the speaker, full of authority his younger self has zero right to assume. "Money and company. It's a win-win, bro."

Win-win? He's out of his mind.

Scowling, I kick the roll of offending lights back into the corner of the attic where they belong and squeeze my way back to the loft hatch. "Fuck's sake, will you give it a rest? Pour l'amour de dieu."

For the love of god.

Or at least for the love of me.

But Sab doesn't care about any of that—God, or annoying me enough that I jam an unlit smoke between my lips and think hard about lighting it. He *likes* annoying me. To him, it's an

Olympic sport, and I know he won't quit until he takes a medal.

He's still talking. I block him out as I pick through another box of junk, searching for the *white* lights I came up here for. The cute warm ones I need for the Instagram post I don't give a fuck about. The *essential* post I have to make to keep my account visible enough to keep my actual lights on, in the house I can't afford to live in without taking Sab's advice.

Which is why I've already taken it, but he doesn't need to know that. Not yet, anyway. Sab's persistent. Like a fucking rash. But he's not the most stubborn Dubois brother. That title is *mine* and I'm not giving it up anytime soon.

"...maybe you need to get laid."

I tune back in to that beauty. "Tu me fais chier. Fuck off with that shit."

Sab does not fuck off. He treats me to another twenty minutes of underlining how boring I am these days and how shit my life is, disregarding every attempt I make to tell him the opposite. That I'm fucking happy living alone and I don't give a damn if his secondhand view of my existence tells him otherwise. By the time he's done, I'm glad I haven't told him my unwelcome lodger is moving in tomorrow. Let him walk into my house and find a stranger at the table we grew up around.

Except the lodger I haven't yet met won't be in my house. He'll be in the annex, using the side gate as an entrance because I don't want someone—*anyone*—all up in my shit. Not even Sab, who's still aggravating me enough I hang up on him.

A text pings through a moment later and I realise he's changed my notification tone from a nondescript beep to the opening chords of Jingle Bells set at top volume.

It's loud enough to rattle my brain and make the dog bark

3

from his spot on the couch downstairs, but I ignore him, searching for the elusive lights. They have to be up here somewhere. My whole life is crammed into this tiny space since I cleared out my studio to make room for a lodger I don't even want. A lodger I *need* if I'm going to make next month's mortgage payment without starving to death. A distant dream if I don't pick up more seasonal work, which means the Instagram post I'd rather stick pins in my eyes than create is more important than ever.

If I can just find these fucking lights.

They're not with the rest of the Christmas crap I'm not feeling festive enough to face yet. I abandon the attic in favour of the garage, which takes me past the goddamn space I gave up for a lodger I've only communicated with through the letting agent handling his lease.

I know his name. Probably. It's on a letter I've left somewhere by the front door. But denial is a wicked thing, and I've spent the last few months fooling myself the less I know about the looming change in my life, the less real it is. Except, it's really fucking real—it's happening *tomorrow*, and it's not going anywhere until the lease runs out in six months' time.

Six months.

The agent called it a short lease, but to me, it feels like a lifetime. Years ago, I was the kind of dude who rolled with the tides. These days, I find all the joy I need in stability and giving it up feels like the end of the world.

At least, it does while I'm scrabbling around the garage. It's worse than the attic, and it's *cold*, a state of affairs that never cheers me up. Makes me wonder why I'm fighting so hard to be here when my parents spend their days chasing the sun around the Med. But I was born here—*Sab's* here, and however annoying he is, this is where I'll stay.

If I survive tearing through my garage. I have scars on my body that throb in the winter, but this place is a death trap. Teetering piles of wood, scrap metal, and motorbike parts—leftovers from my old life I never got round to ditching.

You didn't want to.

But I regret that now I spot the box of lights behind a vast stack of unfinished worktops, lurking beside a squashed Christmas tree—a plastic one that must be Sab's, because I'd die before I had that shit in my house. I like the smell of the real ones. The piney fir scent that reminds me of my Scottish nan and the weird cannonball cake she used to make on Christmas Eve. Can't remember eating it. Just that Sab stole it one year and lobbed it at my head, missed and broke a window.

The lights.

My brother's face fades out, taking his laughter and leaving me with the urgency that brought me into the dusty garage in the first place. I'm unimpressed by the effort it's going to take to reach them, but the thought of living through a day like this all over again in six months' time, when the old tenant moves out and a new one moves in, propels me into action.

I lent my ladder to an old friend and never got it back. I go back inside for shoes—I work from home, sometimes I forget my feet are bare—and prod the dog on my way past, checking he's alive.

Rudy rumbles a warning, but he's the size of a bloated gerbil, so I take my chances and poke him again, standing my ground until he rolls over, showing me his belly. "You're all fucking bark, son, ain't ya?"

Course he is, but he makes enough noise that the postman

thinks he's a Rottie, and I'm here for it, even as he bursts from the couch to raise bloody murder at a passing car. Although, this time, he might have a point.

I straighten, tracking the old VW as it slows, the driver easing down the window to peer at my front door.

It should alarm me. I'm a good boy these days, but I wasn't always. And I used to live the kind of life where a drive-by attack wasn't something that just happened on TV. But it's been a long time, six fucking years, and I'm off my game—off my guard, and easily distracted by the face of the hottest dude I've seen since my ex FWB paid me a platonic visit a few weeks back.

My view of the hot dude is brief. Just enough to catch the shock of dark blond hair and killer cheekbones. Eyes that seem blue, though I can't be sure, and a forearm that even hidden by a bomber jacket I know is some kind of perfect.

Merde. I don't think in French that often—only when I'm around Sab and he's pissing me off. Or I'm drunk as a skunk, or deep in my feelings. But it's the only word that comes to me as the car moves off, leaving me dry-mouthed and breathless. As if I've never seen a hot bloke before. As if I'll never see one again. At least not one that matches up to him.

Avoir le coup de foudre.

I snort at myself. I felt that with Rudy last Christmas—love at first sight, and look where it got me? Butler to an angry hamster that bites my ankles when I don't feed him quick enough.

Still, it takes effort to tear my gaze from the window. To reanimate and stamp into my boots. To *remember* I have a purpose in life beyond wondering who Blondie is, and why he was eyeballing my house.

I go back to the garage. Rudy follows and turns his gaze

upward, already stink-eyeing the lights. My dog hates everything Christmas, except the real tree I don't have yet and the food he'll get to steal. It's early *November*, which makes dicing with death for an Instagram post even more of an absolute piss-take. And I'd give it up if I had a choice. But I don't. I need the extra money the cheesy post might bring in, and if I have to climb the shoddy metal racking to get it, that's what I'll do.

Under Rudy's watchful gaze, I root a boot to the bottom shelf and haul myself up. I'm in pretty good shape for the mess I was in six years ago, and I like the burn in my shoulders as my arms take my weight. The wobble and groan of the racking isn't my favourite thing, but I make it work and reach around the squashed Christmas tree to snag the lights.

Relief surges through me. I shimmy down, taking care not to jostle the clusterfuck I've left behind. But I'm not careful enough. My boots touch the floor and an ominous rumble sounds above me. I look up in time to see the stacked worktops listing and they tumble on top of me before I can lurch out of the way.

Rudy.

That's my first thought.

My second, after I realise he's safe in the doorway turns the air blue, French and English pouring out of me in a brutal blend of *motherfucker, that hurt*. Really hurt, everywhere from my fingers to a shoulder that's already been through the wars.

Merde. I mean it this time, with my fucking soul. I shove the heavy wood out of the way and free my arm, flexing my fingers. They barely move, and my thumb joint cops the worst as fresh pain infiltrates my wrist.

Goddammit.

I leave the lights and traipse inside. Rudy shadows me,

growling as I re-examine my arm in the kitchen, using the stove lights to stave off the fading winter sun outside.

I'm bleeding. My hand trembles, and I know it's bad. That I should go to the urgent care centre in town, or even the hospital in the city. But...I don't want to. Something inside me freezes and I'm out of fucks for one day. Or maybe I'm running short on the courage it takes to walk into a building I left so much of myself in so many years ago.

Either way, I'm not going. Stubborn, remember? And I'm a fucking idiot. So I turn the lights off and lie down on the couch, shutting my eyes, cradling my wrist to my chest and leaning into a hard avoidance nap, something I'm good at.

And who knows? I'm not the luckiest fucker in the world, but maybe the last ten minutes were nothing but a shittastic dream. Maybe the last six months were too, and my imminent lodger is a Christmas nightmare I won't have to live with after all.

BHODI

I've always had terrible timing. Everything that ever happens to me seems to play out at the worst possible moment, and the HDU night shift I'm about to walk into is no exception. Honestly, who picks Sunday night graveyard hours to start a new job?

Me, that's who. Bloody genius, mate. The same *idiot* who drove four hours from Cornwall to Hereford in an aging Golf that desperately needs an oil change. If I had a brain, I'd be dangerous.

Not fair. You're tired and emotional.

Valid. But I've made these mistakes when I'm happy too, so I can't blame my predicament on being a little bit knackered and nursing a bruised heart.

My car's had enough of me for one day. I secure it a reserved space that's going to cost me a ridiculous wedge each month and pick my way through the frosty car park—a concrete abyss with the same miserable vibe of every hospital I've ever worked in. And I've worked in a few. *More than a few.* Putting roots down isn't my forte, and if the last few months—the last *year*—has taught me anything, it's that my regular trick of legging it when things go wrong has more merit than sticking around to get shat on.

He didn't shit on you. It's not his fault you caught feelings he didn't reciprocate.

Skylar.

My ex.

At least, that's how I see it. To him, I'm just a hookup that fizzled out.

Still not his fault.

I know that. I *know* it. But it doesn't make the sigh rattling my chest any lighter. The ache in my chest any less potent. And I don't like it. It's why I need to be *here*, in this unfamiliar place, starting over for the hundredth time. Because if there's one thing worse than being dumped, it's the sound knowledge that the dumper has barely noticed you're gone.

It's a reality that weighs heavy on me, and it shouldn't. Skylar's a nice person—messed up, but nice. Honest. He told me from the start he was only up for NSA sex, but my stupid heart didn't hear him. And that's what I need to take from this

—my umpteenth stroll into a brand new place: the next time someone tells me they're just down to fuck, *listen*.

Or at least, get in there first. I like sex. And I like not getting hurt. On the off-chance I'm ever brave enough to get nekkid with someone again, I'm setting the boundaries.

The utter brilliance of my internal monologue brings me within sight of the hospital's main entrance. A huge set of double doors that will take me to the third floor and the HDU ward I'll be haunting for the next six months. A temporary contract I signed in the dead of night when I'd drunk too much cider and melancholy. To get there, I need to cross the throughway and pass the A&E department which is already spilling out into the taxi ranks and ambulance bays.

I weave through a couple of drunks, about to cross the road, but a lone figure ahead of me catches my attention. A dude with his arm cradled to his chest who nears the A&E doors and abruptly veers away, heading back to the far side of the car park.

I'm pushed for time, and I've already wasted most of my day washing my clothes in a local laundrette so I don't roll up to my new place in the morning rocking hobo vibes. But my gaze follows the man as he comes to a stop and hunches over, bowing his head, and staying my course to the looming double doors ahead is a wrench my soft heart can't handle.

I dig the hospital ID I picked up a few weeks back from my jacket and let it hang loose against my chest. Then I veer off-piste and stay on the wrong side of the road, catching the tall bloke up as he rotates to lean against a lamp-post, glaring at the misty sky.

The motion makes the hood he's wearing slip back, revealing his face, and my pace falters, my whole body stuttered by the scruffy perfection of his profile.

Shaggy hair.

Unshaven jaw.

A face tattoo that's too small and intricate for me to make out, and eyes that gleam in the dark, like a wolf in the forest.

They might be brown, his eyes, but in the murky light, it's hard to tell, and I'm close enough by now that staring is going to get me in trouble. This fella—he's pretty—*so pretty*—but there's an edge to him I've seen in beautiful men before, and I rein myself in, playing nurse instead of creeper, wondering if he's one of the homeless men I've seen sleeping under the bridge. "You all right there, mate?"

Slowly, the man lowers his gaze, gifting me a full view of his face. Of the messy dark hair that falls to his chin, and the tiny ink that simmers below his left eye. "What?"

I gesture to the arm he's still holding to his chest. "Are you okay?"

He stares, a minuscule frown pleating his brows. As if he's trying to place me, when I know he can't. There's no way we've set eyes on each other before. No *way*. I'd remember this bloke in a coma. I'd remember his *voice* as he clips a single syllable at me. "Yeah."

It takes me a second to remember what I asked him. Then to see through the lie.

The arm he's holding, it isn't strapped, and there's dried blood on his fingers. More than that, as searingly attractive as he is, it takes more than a hard gaze to hide the kind of pain I spend my working life confronting. This man...he's a lot of things. But in this moment *okay* isn't one of them.

"Have you been triaged inside?"

"What?"

"Triaged." I try again. "So a doctor can look at that arm."

Seconds tick by, and I begin to think he won't answer. That I'll have to walk away on the weakness of his first response and spend the rest of the night pondering his fate.

It's a road I've travelled before, but as I resign myself to it, something seems to shift and he sighs. "Honestly, I'm fucking fine. Just banged up a bit, but it's better already."

He gifts me the smallest half grin, and it's almost enough to dazzle me into believing him, but I don't believe him. Not even close. He has no intention of going inside, but the fact that he didn't keep walking before I reached him is clue enough that he knows he should.

I try a different tack. "What happened?"

"Something fell on me."

"What was it?"

"French oak."

"A big bit?"

"Lots of big bits." The man appraises me, taking in the scrubs I'm wearing and the ID I pried free of my jacket. "You work here?"

"Nah, I just like the clothes."

His smile almost widens. But whatever's got hold of him tonight tightens its grip and his humour fades. "I need to go. I left my dog alone."

He retreats a little, and it should be my cue to let it go. But I don't move. And for long moments, neither does he, and it feels like we know each other. Or as if we should. But feelings like this—they're clouds, floating on by, and the reality that we're strangers in the dark is hard to ignore.

I step back.

He nods and spins around, walking away. He doesn't look back and it feels right.

Until it doesn't. But that doesn't hit me until I'm walking away too, and by then, I'm late to the twelve-hour shift I have to get through before I move into a property I haven't seen, attached to the house of someone I've never met, and I don't have the headspace for a handsome enigma.

But the thing is, my heart might be on lockdown, but my brain has other ideas, and I know this dude will be on my mind for the rest of the night.

And for whatever reason, I'm okay with that.

Two

BHODI

I'm less okay with it, and pretty much everything else, by the time the morning rolls around. Night shifts suck, and navigating a new place made this one more intense than I'm used to after sticking it out in Truro longer than I ever have anywhere else.

New people.

New protocols.

New *green* scrubs that remind me of the slime a toddler once puked on me in A&E too many years ago to count.

I shouldn't be thinking about puke. I'm hungry. But I climb into my car with a brain like sludge and it's hard to contain.

Fighting with *Maps* distracts me. I punch in the postcode for my new digs, grateful I took the time for a drive-by the day before, just to check the road name was real.

Stardust Lane.

Sounds magical, but the way my luck has gone recently, I

bet it's a dump. Serves me right for signing a lease without viewing the studio flat attached to it first, but that's my life. It's how I roll, and I'll roll with this until it's over.

My phone finally plays ball. I point my car north, out of the city and into the sticks, and pray I'll stay awake all the way to my new home.

A dangerous game. One I've seen the consequences of too many times to play fast and loose with the road. But it's a short journey, and I make it to Stardust Lane before fatigue eats me whole, and ditch my car next to the road sign I spotted yesterday.

Like everything else, it's covered in frost. And I stagger out of my car to the tiniest snowflakes falling from the dawn sky. If I wasn't delirious with exhaustion, I'd hold my hands out and spin around. But as it goes, it takes all my energy to grab a bag from the boot of my car and shuffle for the lock box where the letting agent promised I'd find my keys.

"The landlord wants to keep things separate from his living space. Chances are, you'll never see him."

Suits me. I'm a people person when my mood's right. But night shifts suck the life out of me. I need a bed to fall face-first into. I'll worry about avoiding my reclusive landlord later.

I retrieve the keys and navigate to the side gate. It's secured by another combination lock and it takes me a second to recall the code. Then it sticks, and I have to shake the gate to open it.

The commotion is louder than the frosty sunrise glittering over Stardust Lane deserves, and it wakes a dog somewhere.

Somewhere *close*. I shove the gate open as the deep bark reaches the fence and cringe. If this is me every morning for the next week, my landlord is going to *love* me.

The barking gets louder. I shut the gate and follow the path to a white building I assume is where I live now. I get my key in the lock, seconds from being blessedly inside, but as the lock clicks, all hell breaks loose.

Hell in the body of the smallest, cutest dog I've ever seen.

It bursts through the fence, taking a panel with it, and hurls itself at my legs, still barking up a storm. If it wasn't so small, I'd be scared, but it's no bigger than an angry squirrel and I laugh, letting it do its thing while I wince at the wrecked fence.

"Didn't like that panel, eh?"

The dog jumps again. This time I crouch to meet it and realise it's vibrating with excitement more than violence, though it still sounds like it wants to eat me.

"Rudy!" Hurried footsteps sound beyond the hole in the fence. "*Rudy*—Putain de merde. What the fuck happened here?"

I raise my gaze from the dog, startled by the deep voice that rakes the air in English *and* French. By the biker boots that appear by the bag I've dropped, and the long, denim-clad legs they're attached to.

Tattooed arms, one cradled to a strong chest. And a set of wide russet eyes that hold the same shock and awe I feel. "Fuck. It's you."

I rise, half convinced the night shift I've just worked is spilling over into a fatigue-laced hallucination. Mostly convinced, actually, as I can't think of a rational explanation for the beautiful, injured man from last night to be standing in front of me in his *pyjamas*.

If you can call low-slung faded sweats, biker boots, and an *open* zip-up hoodie pyjamas.

I'm clutching the dog. I hand it over. He takes it with his

uninjured arm and it's the sight of his fractured wrist that drags words from my throat.

"You didn't go back then?"

"Back where?"

"To A&E. For an X-Ray."

The dog squirms. The man sets him down, watching him scamper through the fence before he looks at me again and profound confusion knits his brows. "Why are you here?"

A fair question. Doesn't answer mine, but it's a start. "I live here." I incline my head to the keys dangling from a door I've yet to open. "Just moving in."

Those pretty eyes widen again. "You're Bhodi Jones?"

He knows my name. My heart skips a ridiculous beat, and I realise there's a chance I might know his. "That's me. Don't suppose you're Tam Dubois, are you? Because that would make you my landlord."

I'm laughing as I say it. *Not homeless then.* But stunned silence answers me. Those *eyes*, and oh. *Oh.* No way. This stuff never happens to me. Closest I've ever come to a rom-com moment was that time Skylar asked me to be his fake boyfriend for a hot second, to stop a nurse in ICU sending him boob pics, and I didn't see him for a month after that.

The dejection that brought me here smothers my amusement, and my companion—*Tam*, though he's yet to confirm it—finally recovers. He shoves his hair out of his face with an inked hand and shakes his head, muttering in French before one phrase sneaks through. "Fucking hell."

I agree. But I'm also hungry, tired, and so poleaxed by how gorgeous he is that I'm struggling to string a sentence together. I need to unlock this door and drag my corpse to bed before I'm capable of the conversation this wild moment deserves. "I thought you were lying about the dog."

"Nope." Tam Dubois reanimates for real and swipes my bag from the ground as the menace in question reappears. "Morphing into a battering ram is a new one, though."

He holds out the bag. It's my cue to take it and unlock the door, but as his faculties return, mine abandon me. I'm rooted in place as he lets the bag slip to his elbow and reaches around me to open the door.

The dog darts inside.

Tam curses and it brings me to my senses.

I rotate and catch my first glimpse of my new home. Blink and take another look, startled all over again by the rustic perfection that greets me. I mean, I read the letting agent's description a month ago, but I'd been drinking, *moping*, and too caught up in what I was leaving behind to move forward with any tangible focus. Definitely do not remember shiny wooden floors. A log burner. Or a couch that takes up most of the living space in the open plan annex.

"Sorry it's small," Tam gruffs from somewhere behind me. "And that it's already covered in dog hair."

His dog zooms around the space, chasing a gold-flecked pipe cleaner. "Are you sure he's not a cat? He's acting like one."

"He's a little shit. Rudy. Come here."

Rudy ignores him.

I venture further into my new house and whistle, but that does no good either and Tam sighs.

"Do you mind if I come in and get him?"

"Have at it. It's your place."

"Actually, it's yours. I put *no inspections* in the contract so I have no right to come in while you're living here."

News to me. Last place I lived the landlord poked his head in so often I probably needed a restraining order against him. But I can't lie and say I'm relieved Tam won't be around the whole time I'm here.

"The landlord wants to keep things separate from his living space. Chances are, you'll never see him."

"You can come in." I shuffle out of the way. "Whenever you want. I don't mind."

Tam slips me an inscrutable glance as he steps over the threshold and toes his boots off. He has tattooed feet and perfect toes, and I can't even...

How is this the world I've woken up to when I haven't been to sleep yet?

"Rudy. *Dégage*. Come on."

This dog. Despite the stern authority lacing a voice that could charm honey from bees, he doesn't give a toss. It's like he wants me to die right here watching his master manoeuvre his wet dream of a body around this gorgeous space, all the while cursing in French. Like he knows it'll be a perfect death.

Trouble is, if I die, then I'll never get to examine Tam's injured wrist, and if I'm certain of nothing else right now, it's that he has no intention of taking it to anyone else.

Instant expert, are you?

No. Not even close. But that wrist. It's bothering me, and unless he's made of stone, it has to be bothering him.

Rudy skids past me.

I lunge and snatch him up. Without his tiny claws scrabbling on the wood floor, the silence is deafening. The clarity—that it's silly o'clock in the morning and I'm sharing oxygen with my landlord, a man who past-me had pegged for a vagrant, who also happens to be a bare-chested smoke show.

An injured smoke show.

I can't let it go. I tuck Rudy under my arm, taking him hostage. "You can have him back if you let me take a look at your wrist."

Tam stops mid-step, already reaching for his dog. "Excuse me?"

He has don't-fuck-with-me vibes for days, but I stand my ground. He can't punch me and grab his dog with one hand, so he has to make a choice, and I make an educated guess that he loves his dog more than he loves himself.

"My wrist is fine."

"Then it won't take long."

"What are you? A doctor or something?"

"Nurse. If it's broken, I can't help you."

"Then why look?"

"Could be a sprain."

"Then what?"

I shrug, out of energy to blag him with. We both know it's not a sprain. I can see the swelling and deformity from where I stand, and the drawn lines on his handsome face give away that he's spent all night feeling it for himself, a notion that squeezes my heart all over again.

It's what makes me a good nurse and a bad one. That I care when maybe I shouldn't. That I can walk away from my own problems without looking back, but someone else's force me to my knees.

Skylar...

No. I don't want to think about him right now. I *can't*, or I'll drown in this fresh start before it gets the chance to save me, and I'm tired of feeling lost. I'm tired of everything.

"All right."

I blink to find Tam has edged close enough that I smell woodsmoke and cinnamon dancing on his olive skin. His eyes are fixed on his dog, vindicating my decision to swipe him, but I can tell by the set of his jaw that he wants to show me his wrist as much as he wants to stick his head in the log burner.

Shame for him, I don't care. I mean, I do. Taking his agency from him is the last thing I want. But my job, wherever I land, is a parade of worst-case scenarios. An untreated fracture can kill a man, and I've seen it happen, so I put Tam's dog down and reach for his wrist.

His frayed sleeves are already rolled back. I take his hand and turn his arm, assessing both sides, palpating the swollen flesh, testing the movement in his fingers.

"Any numbness?"

Tam grunts. "No."

"How's the pain?"

"Fine."

"And when I do this?" I press my thumb harder into the worst of the swelling.

Tam hisses, wrenching his arm away. "All right. You made your point. I know it's fucked."

"Fractured," I correct. "Easily fixed with a cast."

If he's lucky, and doesn't leave it so long it needs re-breaking and setting.

I open my mouth to say so, but he's already snatched Rudy and made it halfway to the open door.

He's done, I realise, and I have to respect it. But not without telling him the truth. "You can't ignore an injury like that. If it heals wrong, you'll need surgery to correct it."

"Nice to meet you." Tam steps into his boots and leaves, shutting the door behind him with a quiet click.

His departure is so abrupt I go back to believing I fell asleep on the way home and I've yet to wake up. But his scent lingers, the warmth of his bare skin against my palms. The fluff from his crazy dog.

I'm in his house.

I mean, not literally. I'm in an annex he owns, that he's renting to me on a short-term lease under the condition he never has to deal with me, and I've pushed myself all up in his face twice in the past twelve hours.

But still. My tiny mind is blown and it makes it hard to take in the lush space I've somehow landed in.

The sofa.

It's a bed—I remember that much from the emails. It folds out, creating a bedroom in the living area that holds a tiny kitchen, and a separate bathroom tucked into the back.

The rest of the space is all wood and huge windows, natural light pooling as the sun grows stronger. The log burner I'm too tired to investigate, and a rug big enough to—

Nope.

I get horny when I'm tired. Like my body knows a good fuck would gift me the best sleep ever. It makes going to bed alone depressing, but I'm too far gone to care right now. I'm not even hungry anymore. I'm just going through the motions, booting my shoes and losing my coat, dumping it on the floor as I wrestle with the sofa-bed.

It springs out on the third try. There's bedding in my car, but I don't care enough to fetch it. Everything is tomorrow's problem. *Tonight's*, when I wake up and go back to work.

Exhaling, I flop onto the bed and let my gaze sweep the annex one last time. It's clean, but not too clean, the dust that remains homely, not grotty, and there's tinsel hanging from the beam above me, as if someone forgot to put it away last year. In the winter sun, it's so gold it's almost bronze, and it makes me think of Tam's russet gaze, and the kaleidoscope of emotion I've seen in him since we set eyes on each other last night.

Still doesn't feel real. Any of it. But this bed, it smells of him, and as I crash into a deep sleep, it feels like he's still here.

Three

TAM

I was right about his eyes. They're blue and jewel-bright. Full of life and laughter, even though every time I see him, he's trudging to his front door as if he's been awake for a week and a half.

He's on nights.

Bhodi Jones.

AKA the hot bloke who lives in my annex.

AKA the hot nurse from the hospital car park.

AKA the thunderbolt driver I'd clocked the day before he got here.

Three strikes of coincidence that blow my mind, but I haven't had time to think about much. Not since the Instagram post that smashed up my wrist worked its magic and I have a dozen new orders to complete by the last post in December.

And to be clear, just because I haven't had time to think about Bhodi Jones and his electric eyes, doesn't mean I haven't done it anyway. My wrist hurts and picturing his face dulls the pain. Also, I can see him from the spare room window because that beautiful fucker never closes the blinds when he sleeps during the day and I'm too weak not to stare.

Like now, as I rise to refill the ink pot I've been working with—a task that's a pain in the arse now I'm working up here, instead of *down there*, where he's passed out on top of the covers, his pale arm dangling off the side of the bed, his messy blond hair and cut torso—

Stop it.

Honestly, I'm trying. But he doesn't make it easy, and it drives me to wonder how I'd have spent the last three days if I hadn't had so much work to do. If I'd have stared at him *more*.

You're his landlord. Be-fucking-have.

I raid my ink stash for a fresh pot of holly-berry red and return to my table. My wrist throbs something rotten. It hasn't turned black and fallen off yet, but fuck me, it hurts, and if I take any more ibuprofen I'll give myself a fucking ulcer. A cold fact that makes it harder to believe the injury will magically heal itself, but it's all I have until my brain unknots.

Keep busy.

Right.

Work.

I go back to handcrafting place cards for the town mayor's Christmas ball. Red and green custom calligraphy. Easy money, but dull, and if I have to write one more double-barrelled toff name, I'm gonna grind my pen nib into my eyeball.

Maybe.

If I don't get derailed pondering what time my lodger is going to wake up today. Or fretting that he might be cold. He hasn't lit the burner and the weather has turned lethal since he arrived a few days ago. Frost on the grass, ice on the roads. It's hard to believe it rained for two weeks straight before he got here.

Actually, it's hard to believe he *is* here. That if he wasn't so distractingly hot, having a lodger would have zero impact on my life, just like Sab said.

I should've done this years ago.

Oh well.

Stealing glances at Bhodi, I work all morning. Then I go outside and contemplate the fence my mouse-sized dog somehow managed to destroy in his eagerness to get to Bhodi. I mean, now I've seen him up close and felt his warm hands on my skin, I get it. But that doesn't help me fix the fence with one working hand.

I'm still glaring at it when Sab calls. "What?"

"Grinch."

"What do you want?"

"How are you in a mood already? C'est à peine l'heure du déjeuner."

It's barely lunchtime. "I'm not in a mood."

"You've been in a mood for *days*. Hang on…"

He ends the call and FaceTimes instead. I roll my eyes, but I know better than to ignore him, and I don't want to. Sab's my best friend. If anyone can screw my head back on, it's him.

Somehow, I forget that means he also sees straight through me in less than a second. "What's wrong with you? Did you die twice since I last came down?"

It's a bad joke, but we've been rolling with it for six long years, and it lacks the punch it once had. "Nothing's wrong."

"C'est des foutaises." *Bullshit.* Sab leans forward. He's in the big van—*my* van. The oversized heap of junk he won't get rid of in case I ever want it back. "What happened?"

I open my mouth to repeat the lie, but Rudy interrupts me, kicking up a racket at a delivery driver picking his way up the path to the main gate. The little shit is ferocious enough that the driver hesitates, but I need the canvas boards he's carrying for the job in my diary for tomorrow, and my schedule's packed enough now that I don't have time to chase missing parcels.

"Hang on."

That's for Sab. The toe of my boot is for Rudy as I gently nudge him into the house, shutting him in.

He's unimpressed—Rudy, I don't know about Sab. But they both have to wait as I meet the driver halfway, reaching for the boards before I remember that I can't fucking hold them.

The driver sees my predicament and helps me out, carrying them to my front door for me to retrieve one by one when Rudy isn't doing his nut. But every silver lining has a cloud and I don't have to look at my phone to know my nosy brother has heard every word I've exchanged with the friendly Evri man.

I cage a sigh as the driver returns to his van and retreat to the garden again, hoping I can distract Sab with the broken fence, but he's not having it.

"What happened to your arm?"

"Nothing."

"Liar."

"Am I?"

"Oui-oui." Sab has the same dark brows as me. They pull together as he launches into a tirade of irritated French, calling me out for being exactly who I am.

When he's done, I throw him a bone to shut him up. "I knocked it a bit in the garage."

"How? When?"

I don't feel like explaining the daft chain of events that led to the *probable fracture* I'm walking around with—Bhodi's words, not mine. Or dealing with the frustration Sab's going to inflict on me when he figures out I haven't had it treated yet. The humiliating empathy when he figures out *why*.

You're ridiculous.

I am, and I know it, as much as I *know* I'm running out of rope to put it right. But this shit—unpicking the mess in my head—it takes time, and doing it alone is hard. If Sab was here...

He can't be. He's got an actual child to take care of, remember?

"Look, don't worry about it, okay? It's fine."

"He's lying."

I spin around. Bhodi's behind me, on the steps of the annex, dressed for work six hours before I'm expecting him to leave for the night. Because after three days of watching him sleep off his night shifts, I've somehow convinced myself I know his routine. "I'm not lying."

Bhodi grunts and moves past me, heading for the side gate I never use, and I have no working free hand to stop him. No *reason* to stop him beyond the fact that he's just dropped me in it with Sab. But the back of his head taunts me, as if I have any right to feel something as he walks away from me, and I bank Sab's outrage for later.

I hang up on my brother. A risky move if I don't want him on my doorstep by dinnertime, but the mood I'm in, I can't be sure I don't want that. That I don't need it if I'm not going to let Bhodi's ominous warning come true.

Bhodi.

I shove my phone into my pocket and track his steps down the path to the gate. It gets to me more than it should that he might be gone already, but he's by his car, scraping ice from the windows, not a scrap of apology in the tough gaze he sends me.

"Brother?"

"That obvious?"

"You look alike and I wish my brother talked to me like that."

"In angry French?"

"Sadly, no." Bhodi flicks scraped ice to the ground. "Raging cockney doesn't have the same magic."

"You're from London?"

"Carmarthen, actually. My brother's ten years older than me."

He doesn't sound Welsh. And my confusion must show on my face as he rounds the back of his car to tackle the rear windshield. "My dad worked on oil rigs. We lived everywhere, so I don't sound like anything."

"That's not true."

"Yeah? What do I sound like, Tam?"

I can't see his face as he wraps his voice around my name, and I'm transfixed by how his jacket rides up, revealing the swathe of ink-free skin I've already mapped out by creeping on him all week. "You sound like a dude who just got me in trouble with my brother."

Bhodi doesn't say anything for a moment. He clears the windshield, keeping his back to me, and the silence, though loaded, doesn't feel bad. If anything, I feel calmer, like being close to him settles something inside me, which is fucking ludicrous. I don't know this dude. He's my *lodger*. The one I have to explain to Sab when he calls back later and rips me a new one.

"How much trouble are you in?"

In my daze, I've missed Bhodi finishing his car and moving closer. He has major bedhead. The kind that makes me want to burrow my fingers into the thick locks and count the colours. "Enough to make me think about chucking my phone off Firefly Hill."

"Firefly Hill?"

I point to the grassy peak in the distance, dotted with only a few homes. In truth, it isn't that high, but the sentiment stands.

Bhodi follows my finger. "The road names are amazing around here."

"They're deceiving. Cosmic Avenue is a shithole."

He grins, and it's a fucking delight. Then his gaze falls on my wrist and seriousness descends on him again. "Show me?"

I'm a stubborn bastard. Instinct has me shaking my head before I've truly grasped the question. But Bhodi reaches for me anyway, and my body betrays me, letting him extend my arm without protest, like it knows how much I need the sweet sensation of his fingers gliding over my skin.

His *cold* fingers this time, that find the pain points in my wrists with lethal precision. "Flex your fingers?"

No. I try. It doesn't go well and Bhodi gives me the good news. "Still fractured. Still needs an X-Ray."

"Still not going."

"You know it's free, right?"

"I have to work."

"With one hand?"

"I'm ambidextrous."

Bhodi narrows his gaze, dimming the light in his eyes. "This is winding me up and I don't even know you. How do you think your brother feels?"

"I don't need to think about it, he tells me."

"What's he going to say when you get an infection in the bone from an untreated fracture?"

I sigh, out of arguments.

Bhodi's expression softens and he rolls down my sleeve to cover my arm, avoiding the sore bits this time and patting my hand for good measure. "Do you have a phobia?"

"Of what?"

"Hospitals. Doctors."

Denial bubbles up my throat and doesn't quite make it out. Instead, I say something worse. "It's complicated."

Bhodi smiles a little—a brief ray of sunshine that leaves me wanting more. "Most things are. But I could come with you...if you want? I know how hospitals operate and sometimes that helps."

I know how hospitals operate too, especially the one where I first laid eyes on him, and I want to tell him that, so he understands, for no tangible reason whatsoever.

But my phone rings, shutting me down, and by the time I've rejected Sab's call, Bhodi is already backing away.

"I have to go."

"To work?"

"Yeah." He opens the car door. "I'm covering the late shift before I have a few rest days."

Odd relief sweeps through me that he's not working all night again, though I can't deny I've grown used to breaking up my own work day with the sight of him passed out on the sofa bed. "How late is late?"

"Midnight, probably. I don't know. I'm still getting used to a new place."

I nod. Somehow I've drifted close enough to rest my good hand on his car door.

Shut it. Let him go. Preferably before he has more to say about my fucked-up wrist. But Bhodi's eyes...I have a festive ink shade upstairs that's been making me think of him all week. It's called *spruce*, and I like it, but it has nothing on the glittery stare that pins me in place now.

We've run out of things to say. I get the message and step back, letting Bhodi close his own door. He starts the car, or tries. The ignition sputters and rattles, protesting—*struggling*—before it begrudgingly sparks to life and Bhodi drives away, leaving me with the diesel fog of an unhappy engine.

I *don't* like that. Any of it. Broken cars are dangerous, and it bothers me more than it should that I won't know until Bhodi comes home that he made it to work okay. That he has to drive that car again, at night and through the ice before I can fall asleep.

It bothers me so much I don't go to bed early like I'd planned. I wait up on the couch and let Sab bully me into agreeing to get my wrist seen the next day, on pain of him marching down from Manchester and sitting on me until I stop being so fucking extra. He's so wound up he doesn't even ask what happened to the fence, who Bhodi was, and why he was rolling out of the annex with bed hair at two o'clock on a Thursday afternoon. Which has its good and bad points. I'm not sad about delaying Sab's smugness over being right about the rental income, but Bhodi's hot, and I can't stop thinking about him, and Sab's my person for talking about this shit.

He's my person for everything.

It's late when Bhodi's car finally pulls up outside. I'm

dozing with my phone on my chest. I sit up and it clatters to the floor as Bhodi exits his car and disappears around the house, using the side gate I had stipulated in his contract, only the battered fence gifting me a snatched glimpse of him again before he vanishes into the annex.

He doesn't turn any lights on, but I don't need to see him to know he's kicking his shoes off and ditching the clothes from his upper body before he fills a glass of water he won't drink and knocks out face-down on his unmade bed.

It's my cue to climb the stairs to my own bed, but I can't make myself move. I lie back on the couch and fold my good arm behind my head, watching the flames in the burner smoulder and die. Something deep inside me is wide awake, and I feel like this is me for the night. That I'll still be at one with the fire when morning comes. But I do fall asleep in the end and wake to Rudy terrorising me for his breakfast, and a note on the doormat.

Rudy waits for no man.

I feed him, then shuffle to the front door and snag the plain card that's definitely one of mine.

It's covered in illegible scrawl, letters squished together and overlapping, words slanting forward and back in wavy lines. It's so early that deciphering it hurts my brain, but the one word I can read—the scribbled name—spurs me on, and eventually, I figure it out.

FRACTURE CLINIC, 10 AM. I'LL DRIVE.
BHODI xx

Damn. Aside from the what-the-fuck notion that the lodger I didn't even want is already ordering me around, I should be fixated on the *I'll drive* part of the cute little note I can't seem to put down. His car's fucked. He's not driving anywhere until I've stuck my head under the bonnet. But that's a given, non-negotiable, and maybe that's why the two little kisses after his name sink their hooks into me instead.

Four

BHODI

He's not going to come.

I tell myself over and over.

As I roll out of bed three hours earlier than I want to. As I shower in the tiny cubicle with the rainfall head, then contemplate the empty fridge and the unused log burner on repeat until it's time to leave—for the appointment I made, unasked, for my landlord.

The *insanely* attractive bloke with the star tattooed on his face who's rejected my concern for his fractured wrist ten times already.

If anything, I approach my car expecting a note tacked to the windscreen telling me to fuck the fuck off, but I'm wrong. I glance up from picking my way along the icy path to find Tam waiting for me, perched on the low wall surrounding his house, and the sight of him slows my steps.

He's got those boots on. But instead of the sweats I've seen him in recently, jeans wrap around his long legs, a dark jacket thrown over a faded, gunmetal grey T-shirt, and *Lord*, I'm not ready for it.

I force myself into motion again. "Wasn't sure you'd show."

Tam stands off the wall, his injured arm still held at an awkward angle. "You grassed me up to my brother. It's him or you."

"I was your first choice?"

His russet eyes do something complex. "I can go on my own. You don't have to come."

I know that. He knows that. But somehow, we're both here.

"Also," he elaborates when I don't speak, "I googled the fracture clinic, and it's in a different building, so..."

So...? But I don't ask. If he wants to share, he will. Or he won't, and that's okay. I point at my car, the windows already cleared of frost and ice. "Let's go."

A beat stretches before he shrugs and heads to the passenger door of my beat-up Golf. He slides into the seat. I do the same and start her up—kinda. It takes a minute and I shoot him an apologetic glance. "Needs an oil change."

He snorts. "It needs glow plugs. And probably new cylinders if you keep driving it like a crazy person without getting it looked at."

"How are you saying that with a straight face?"

Tam gives me a long look, one I can't drown in while I'm reversing around the cul-de-sac to spin the car in the right direction. "Yeah yeah, I get the irony. But I looked at the engine while I was waiting for you, and you really do need glow plugs."

I face forward and spy the oil smears on his hands, even the bad one. There's other marks too—blue, maybe?—that make less sense, and a red that's too vibrant to be blood staining the skin around his nails. "It's cute that you looked at my car."

"Cute?"

"Yeah. But you didn't need to. I was going to take it to Halfords tomorrow."

"Fucking Halfords?" That earns me a growly grunt, and a flurry of muttered French that somehow fits with the subtle Brummie accent Tam has when he sticks to English.

"You don't like Halfords," I surmise, easing my cursed car down Stardust Lane and onto the A-road that leads to the city. "They do something to offend you?"

"They're shite."

"All of them?"

"Unless you're in the market for a bubblegum air freshener."

Tam shifts his attention to nail a glare at an SUV undertaking us. I roll my lips, suppressing a grin as a bump in the road jostles the Jelly Belly air freshener dangling between us. Blueberry, once upon a time, but it probably smells of old scrubs by now. Or whatever junk is lurking in the back of my car with the bags and boxes I've yet to unpack.

"Why are you going this way?"

I chance a glance at Tam. He's scowling at the junction leading to the motorway, and to the best of my knowledge, the city where we'll find the hospital. "Um. Because we're going to the hospital?"

"Yeah, I know that. But why this way? It takes six times as long."

"Then *Google Maps* lied to me."

"Fucking right. Take the scenic route next time."

I wait for him to elaborate.

He doesn't, and I drive on, trying not to sneak glances at his profile, or breathe too much of his woodsmoke and cinnamon scent. He looks like a biker, but he smells like cake, and facing that without breakfast in my belly is a Herculean task. Add in that he's satanically hot, and I'm a lost cause.

There's no way around it. I want to eat him.

But I want him to feel better more than I want to think about fucking him, and I hold onto that as I navigate my way back to a place that already feels like my second home, park in the last staff space, and kill the engine.

Tam hasn't spoken in a while. He doesn't seem particularly tense, but what do I know? This is the fourth time we've met and the longest we've ever been in each other's company. For all I know, he's about to bolt, and despite his injury, I know I have little chance of stopping him.

I take a chance and press my fist to his shoulder. "Ready?"

"Hmm?"

"We're here." I let my fist slip away. "You've got a little time before your appointment, though. If you need a minute."

Tam blinks. "You made me an appointment?"

"Yup." I lean back in my seat, content to wait. "It's quicker than sitting in the walk-in clinic all morning. Figured you had better things to be doing."

Unless his wrist is so damaged it needs surgery, but we're not there yet. We're in my car—the one he opened the bonnet to without a key. The one that's broken, but reparable. Like everything else.

"Fuck it." Tam moves suddenly and gets out of the car.

I recognise the urgency. He's done thinking and he wants it over with. So I follow him, slip ahead, and lead him round the building that seems to unnerve him so much, and to a smaller operation behind it.

The fracture clinic is busy. I put Tam in a seat by the door, and he lets me. Then I do all the talking at the desk for him so he doesn't have to.

I take a form back to him, along with a chewed-up biro. "Fill that in."

He obeys without comment and I settle into my seat, fighting a yawn. I spent way too long last night debating whether to slip that note through his letterbox. Then I got hungry and remembered I still hadn't been shopping, and dreaming about a meal that didn't come in a foam tray had me tossing and turning until it was time to get up.

I need a nap. A long one. Preferably after I've stuffed my face with something not fried.

"I'm not always this extra." Tam's deep voice startles me, speaking over the tinny rendition of Band Aid filtering from a speaker buried somewhere in the low budget decorations above us. He's finished the form and fixed his attention on me instead, his stare swirling with dry self-deprecation, and the warmth that makes him so attractive. "In case you were wondering."

I open my mouth to deny it, but it'd be a lie. "It's not extra to be nuanced. Everyone has something."

"What's your thing?"

"Running away every time things don't work out."

"Girl trouble?"

"Sometimes. It was a dude this time, though."

I force myself to keep my gaze on the screen that calls patients forward for their appointments. To not track his reaction to the man-love thing. If my sexuality makes him uncomfortable, I can't say I care that much.

"He break your heart?"

I turn my head.

Tam's expression hasn't changed except to flare with

sympathy I don't entirely deserve. "Not quite. It was on its way, though. You know when your head signs up for something your heart can't handle?"

His gaze deepens. "Ouch. Yeah. I've been there. It's why I don't do relationships anymore. Or even hookups unless it's with someone I know for sure doesn't want anything else."

"You don't get lonely?"

"So fucking lonely." Tam touches his good hand to his chest. "But I've been broken before, and I don't have the energy to fix myself again."

The declaration feels loaded, as though we're talking about more than love, and that wide awake part of me from last night surges to life.

I lean forward in the same moment Tam shifts a little, rotating to face me better. Like we're in a quiet corner of a cosy pub instead of a bright and noisy hospital waiting room. Like we're old friends, not new acquaintances.

It should feel weird.

It doesn't.

"How long have you been sworn off love?"

"Years." Tam lets his hand drop and it's a struggle not to study the ink on his knuckles while I have him this close. "My brother calls me a bitter old spinster, but then he's here every other week, kipping on my couch because he can't get along with his missus, and I don't feel like I'm missing much."

I can't disagree. It's the same conclusion that led me to up sticks and move two hundred miles. But hearing him saying it, and seeing the certainty in his molten gaze that this is how it's meant to be for him—I don't know. It doesn't sit right. Like a deeper part of me knows this man is meant to be loved.

"Tam Dubois?"

Our cinched gazes break. We've been so wrapped up in our conversation we've missed Tam's name turning green on the screen and the nurse has come to fetch him.

He rises, tension returning to his face.

I catch his hand—by accident, I think. But here we are. "You want me to come?"

Tam hesitates, a myriad of emotions crowding his gaze. Fear. Bewilderment. Frustration. They're gone in a heartbeat, but I see them, and I stand without waiting for an answer.

"Come on, mate. Let's get you fixed up."

Five

TAM

To no one's surprise, not even mine, my wrist is fractured in two places. I get a cast and a bollocking from a doctor for leaving it so long. But I don't need surgery, and Bhodi is with me, so I don't have much to complain about.

Bhodi. He was in the room when the doctor pulled my medical records and mentioned the shit-ton of broken bones I've suffered before, standing behind me, his hands on my shoulders as if we're old friends, not strangers who met for the first time a few nights ago.

He hasn't asked what happened. Or how it's connected to the intense conversation we fell into in the waiting room. The one that made me forget the weird buzz in those old scars and the razed sensation in my gut. It's crazy how he does that—with everything, not just the clusterfuck I dragged into the hospital with me. Five minutes with him and I forget my fucking name.

"We can go now."

I'm not asleep, but I come back into the room like I'm waking from hibernation. "What?"

Bhodi grins and moves closer, rubbing my arm—the one not encased in fibreglass. "You're all done. We can go home, unless you want to extend your nap here."

My desire to hang out at the hospital is less than zero.

I sit up, testing the weight of my casted arm and the flexibility in my fingers.

My arm weighs nothing. My fingers remain utterly fucked, but I can live with that.

Bhodi sets my boots where I can step into them and passes me a paper bag.

A bag that rattles. "What's this?"

"Your prescription. I got it while you were snoozing."

I don't believe him. I hate this place. Everything about it sets my teeth on edge. But *Bhodi*, man. He's a fucking sorcerer. If anyone can chill me to sleep on a hospital bed, it's him, and it's an odd feeling to know it.

We leave the fracture clinic. Bhodi steers his fucked-up car onto the main road. I have every intention of directing him to the garage on Bell Street, but I'm so fucking tired I can't formulate the words, and we're home in no time.

"You should take it easy for a couple of days." He guides me through the gate, hovering on the other side, as if he remembers that his tenancy agreement forbids him from approaching my house. "Do you have someone you can call?"

"For what?"

It's another cold day. Bhodi rests his hands on the frosty gate and gives me a patient look. "To help you out."

I flex my fingers, ignoring the bolt of pain that rockets up my arm. "I don't need help, and I don't have time to kick it. November is my busiest month."

Bhodi sizes me up, probably trying to figure out what I do for a living that makes Christmas so stacked. But he won't get there—no one ever does, and he surrenders after a beat, backing away. "I'm home all day. Shout if you need anything."

He disappears. I hear the side gate open and close, then I catch another flash of him as he passes the gap left by the missing panel, and I feel like I'm seeing that messy blond hair for the first time all over again.

Avoir le coup de foudre.

No.

No.

I don't believe in shit like that, and if I've learned anything today beyond the depths of my own stupid stubbornness, it's that Bhodi doesn't either.

"What's your thing?"

"Running away every time things don't work out."

Still. I find myself staring after him anyway, lost in the memory of every gentle touch he's sent my way, until Rudy splats himself against the living room window, killing the moment—or at least, the moment I've cooked up in my addled brain.

Shaking my head, I take myself inside and swallow some of the pills from the bag. I need to eat so they don't burn a hole in my stomach. The junk food cupboard calls my name, and I have the worst sweet tooth. I stuff a couple of Mr Kipling pies in my face before I pass out on the couch.

It's dark when I wake up, but at this time of year, that means nothing. Could be teatime or midnight, and I don't much care as the urge to peek at the annex sweeps over me.

Don't. And I'm saved from testing my willpower by the angry chirp of my phone.

It's on the floor by the couch and a cold mug of tea. Sab's face fills the screen and for the first time in days, I don't feel the compulsion to hide from him.

I answer the video call and wait for it to connect while I swipe the pie box and the un-drunk tea from the floor with my one working hand. It means I have to leave Sab behind and he's waiting when I come back, scowling up a storm.

"Where did you go?"

"The kitchen." I rescue him from the arm of the couch and take him upstairs, to the makeshift studio I'm still getting used to, forgetting that Sab doesn't know I've set up shop in the spare room. That he doesn't know *why*.

"And where the fuck are you now?"

"Upstairs. What's wrong with you?"

Sab squints at his phone, his frown deepening. "Are you in the house still?"

"Did you see me go outside?"

"Don't be a dick."

It's tempting to string this out, but I know he's worried about me, so I put him out of his misery. "I took your advice and got a lodger. Which meant I had to move the studio inside —like you said. And I hate it, just so you know, like *I* said I would."

Sab blinks, absorbing the influx of information. Then he laughs, loud and obnoxious. "That's why you've been acting shady for weeks? Because you didn't want to admit my idea was genius?"

"It's not genius, it's common sense."

"Why didn't you think of it first, then?"

"I did think of it, I just didn't want to fucking do it. I still don't."

"Why? Is the lodger a creep?"

"No."

That's it—that's all I say. But my brother knows my face as well as his own, and he's all over whatever he sees so fast I do the only thing I can think of to reroute the incoming train.

I hold up my arm, the casted one that despite the nuclear painkillers coursing through my system, still aches like a bitch. "You were right about *this*. It's broken."

Sab takes the bait and I settle in for a lecture that weaves between French and English so chaotically I'm the sole human on the planet with any hope of understanding him. "You're an idiot." He rounds up in English, his Birmingham accent creeping back in. "Next time just cut it off and be done with it."

"Or," I counter. "You could shift all that oak from my garage. Then there won't be a next time."

"Until you find a new way to nearly die. Now tell me about this fucking lodger."

Damn it. Unbidden, my gaze shifts to the window, and to the annex. There's a low light on in the living space, but I can't see Bhodi, and it's just as well. I don't want Sab to see my face if I catch a glimpse of him. I don't have time for that shit in my life, I have a full day's work to catch up on.

"He's a nurse," I answer Sab's question before he reaches through the screen and shakes me. "Works a lot. Hardly home."

"Is he the hot dude from yesterday?"

"What hot dude?" I frown at the last line of script I completed last night. It's a fucking mess. "I don't know any hot dudes."

Sab sees through my bullshit, but he runs out of time to

interrogate me. It's bedtime for his kid and my brother's a good dad. It's why he's in Manchester, living in a town he hates with a missus who only cares about herself, but that's a story for another day.

He ends the call. I let out a slow breath. Relief, but it's laced with something else—probably the loneliness I admitted to Bhodi earlier when I've spent the last six years denying it to Sab. I have friends and I love my job, but this house...it echoes at night, and it gets to me when I spend too much time alone.

Eventually, I figure out I slept most of the day, and I spend the rest of the evening working, standing at my desk, pouring tea and sugar down my throat to stave off the drowsiness from the cute little pills the hospital gave me.

It's a pattern that continues for the rest of the week. I become nocturnal until I get sick of the dark, and the stomach ache the pills leave in their wake.

Monday morning, I chuck them away and take Rudy for an early walk. He chases a cow. I chase him. Then I carry the little bastard the rest of the way home, because my life is ruled by my tyrannical dog, and if nothing else, his hooliganism distracts me from wondering where Bhodi is. Where he's *been* all week for his car to be gone every time I've glanced out of the window.

It's what you wanted, isn't it? A lodger you never see?

Heh. That was before—when the lodgers I'd imagined were a world away from the blond bombshell Bhodi Jones has turned out to be.

Bhodi Jones.

Merde.

Even his name is hot.

That amazing thought completes as I come up on my house. It's still early, winter sun hazing through the trees, frost glittering on the pavements. The street I live on is pretty as fuck, save the godawful noise rattling from the ancient Golf I've been looking out for all week.

He's home.

My heart has no right to skip a beat. But for whatever reason I don't want to contemplate too hard, it does anyway. And maybe, tucked to my chest, Rudy feels it, and that's why he squirms like a motherfucker, barking loud enough to pop my eardrums.

How Bhodi hears over the racket of his fucked engine, I have no idea. And I'm even less certain if the smile he sends my way as he exits the car is for me. I mean, no one has ever smiled at me like this. Or maybe they have. Maybe it's an ordinary smile and the warmth in my belly is from the Naproxen I've been slamming all week.

Either way, it affects me—*he* affects me, and I'm grateful to my bandit dog for providing an unholy distraction.

I lean over the gate and deposit Rudy in the enclosed front garden. He throws himself at the low wall, desperate to get to the busted fence, but he's shit out of luck. For once I'm one step ahead of him and he's stuck where he is for however long I get to be in Bhodi's company. To lose myself in the low laugh he sends my way, and the smile still lighting his face.

He's so hot.

My first thought's a given. My next, not so much.

He's tired.

I can see it in his eyes. They're still dazzling as fuck, but I can't pretend he doesn't look like someone who's just worked all night. "Long shift?"

Bhodi ventures close enough to peer over the gate at Rudy. "Aren't they all?"

"You don't like your job?"

"I love my job. My new boss, not so much."

"Why's that?"

Bhodi reaches down to scratch Rudy's ears. I take a breath to warn him he might lose a finger, but Rudy chooses that moment to show me that Bhodi's one of the rare people he likes, and I feel that. Pretty sure my dog isn't hooked on the arch of Bhodi's pale neck, though. Or the flex in his shoulders as he straightens without answering my question. "You look better."

"Better than what?"

"Better than a dude walking around with untreated fractures. Is it easier to sleep now?"

Course it is. With my arm in a cast I'm not worried about rolling on it in the night and hurting it worse. But I don't feel like telling him I've swapped my pain-fuelled insomnia for cosy daytime naps when he's been up all night doing God's work. So I nod, agreeing, and change the subject. "Your car is still fucked."

Bhodi cringes, lifting a hand to rub the back of his head. "I got as far as ordering glow plugs online, but I haven't had time to YouTube how to fit them."

"YouTube?"

He shrugs. "Can't be that hard."

"It isn't if you have the tools and know your way around a diesel engine. Does that sound like you?"

It's so easy to grin at him.

What I get back is pure magic.

Bhodi *laughs*, louder than he did at Rudy, but with the same mellow resonance, and the sound wraps around me like a fucking hug. "What gave me away? My girly hands?"

I love women, and I love all kinds of men. But despite how pretty Bhodi is, there's nothing feminine about him. He's as tall as I am, with broader shoulders and a bit more muscle packed onto his lean biceps, and this morning, the barest hint of golden scruff shadows his jaw. "The fact that your car has been making that noise for...let me guess, *months*, gave you away, son."

"It hasn't been months..." Bhodi frowns. "Oh fuck. Maybe it has. I don't know. My life's been a bit..."

He gives an absent wave, but I get the picture. My life has been like that too. Some days it still is. "Well, if it helps, I can switch the glow plugs for you." Bhodi opens his mouth, to protest, maybe, I don't fucking know. I speak again before he gets the chance. "Call it a thank you for carting me to the fracture clinic. I lied to you when I said I had grand plans to go. I didn't."

"Why not?"

I want to tell him. He's so easy to talk to that I know unloading on him would be better than therapy. But he's tired. He's worked all night and driven a fucked-up car on icy roads to get home to his bed. My tale of woe can wait. "I'm not going to make you stand out here and listen to that shit. Go to bed. But knock me up when those plugs arrive. I'll be annoyed if you don't."

"Annoyed, eh? What does that look like?"

"Uglier than this." I point an ink-stained finger at my mug and make myself turn away from him to slip through the gate. By the time I glance back, he's halfway to the annex, and I want to call after him. But I can't think of a reasonable reason to keep him from his bed any longer.

So I let him go, and I spend the rest of my day working and fixing the fence. My casted hand is a cumbersome piece of shit, but my fingers have regained enough movement to be useful, and I make the most of it while the frost holds the rain at bay.

It's mid-afternoon when the Evri man knocks with a package for Bhodi. The annex doesn't have its own address. The driver leaves the parcel with me, and it's not hard to deduce it contains the glow plugs he ordered.

Fuck it. I take the box to Bhodi's car and prepare to wrangle open the bonnet to check he's bought the right ones, but as it happens, the Golf is unlocked, and too old and fucked to have rectified that when Bhodi went to bed.

He's *still* in bed—or, at least, on it. On his belly, that flawless back on display, his hands shoved under the pillow. He doesn't move much when he sleeps. I know this because I've caught myself gazing at him a hundred fucking times today, and *that back.* His skin calls to me, the curve of his spine, his broad shoulders. I want to—

Nope.

Not finishing that sentence. He's my *tenant.* Watching him sleep and thinking dirty things about him is probably illegal, and it's definitely fucking immoral.

So I rip open the parcel addressed to him—to Bhodi fucking Jones—and do what has to be done.

It doesn't take long. It's getting dark by the time I'm finished, but I don't let myself glance at the annex to see if Bhodi's still sleeping.

I go inside and gather Rudy and a giant box of local deliveries, enough to keep me busy till well into the evening. It's late when I get home and Bhodi is gone. But I wake the next morning to another illegible note on the doorstep, and it feels better than any no-strings sex ever has.

BHODI

Tam fixed my car.

While I slept.

The first I knew about it was the Evri man's photo of Tam's boots, and the newly gentle purr of the Golf's engine, but I'd been running too late to thank him in person, and I haven't seen him since. Another pile of night shifts have seen to that, a brutal schedule I volunteered for to make nice with the new team, but by the end of my second week, I'm over it. The senior nurse can't read my handwriting, the vending machines are shit, and I hate the green scrubs.

I mean, I don't. I'm just knackered, and covering a day shift on my first rest day doesn't help, but that's life—*my* life, and I'm beginning to regret everything about it, from the bad sandwich I picked for lunch to the scruff I ran out of time to shave from my jaw.

It's hard to regret Stardust Lane, though. It doesn't seem to matter what time I come home, day or night, it's still the prettiest place I've ever lived.

Landlord's not bad either.

True story, and I find myself looking for Tam as I pull up outside his house, but the small van I've assumed to be his is gone, and there's no rabid dog pelting around the garden. He's out and I curse myself for being disappointed. For the tiny shoot of desire in my belly threatening to bloom into full-blown attraction. I'm sworn to a life of uncomplicated sex, and I don't think lusting after my landlord counts.

Also, I need to go shopping. My cupboards are still bare and the thought of more noodles and chips is enough to put me off dinner altogether.

I take a shower and rinse the day away, stick a load of washing in the machine, then head out again, committed to adulting for just a couple more hours when all I want to do is sleep, and forget that I spent most of my day nursing a patient who ultimately went back to ICU and died ten minutes before I got off shift.

I'm no stranger to losing patients, but it was my first one here, and it stings. I thought she'd live.

She didn't.

"Hey."

I startle, head jerking up seconds before I crash into a lean, tall body that smells of woodsmoke and cinnamon. "Fuck. Hey."

Tam grins. "Sleepwalking again?"

Denial bubbles up my throat but it's beaten by a yawn. "Probably. Where've you been?"

I notice too late that sounds like I've been tracking his comings and goings. That I don't really care manifests much quicker. I like Tam. It's not a crime to be interested in his day-to-day life...right?

"Deliveries." Tam nods to the van. "I needed to clear the decks before I start new orders."

"Orders? Has this got something to do with the oak you dropped on yourself?"

"I didn't drop anything—it fell. And no. I don't do much heavy lifting these days."

I'm so hungry. I need to blow through Tesco, buy some legitimate food that's not laden with salt and MSG before I fall asleep where I stand. But curiosity overpowers the weight of a bad shift, and I realise the craving to know more about him is stronger than the need to eat pasta alone and brood over the patient I lost today. "So what *do* you do?"

Sounds like a come-on. Tam's brows twitch, like he's fighting a smirk, and it's the best thing I've seen all day. All week. Possibly ever. "I do lots of things, but if you're asking about my job, it's probably easier to show you some time than explain."

I want him to show me now, but my stomach chooses that moment to growl so loud it probably scares the birds from the trees. "Sorry." I rub my empty belly. "I need to go food shopping before I expire."

Tam's brows knit for real this time. "You have no food?"

"I have food," I clarify, though his immediate concern is cute. "Just nothing I want to eat after a run of night shifts. I need something hot—like a cuddle on a plate, you know?"

"Like chicken?"

"Maybe."

"Bacon?"

"Stop." Another growl rumbles from my gut. "If I get too hungry, I'll tap out and buy another Pot Noodle multipack."

"Nah. Not happening." Tam moves suddenly and grabs my arm, towing me towards his gate before I find the faculties—or let's face it, the *will*—to protest.

I'm at his front door before I know what's happening. "Are you abducting me?"

"I'm *feeding* you." Tam unlocks his door and kicks it open. His crazy dog rockets down the hallway to greet us, and just like that, I'm in his house.

And he's still holding my arm.

He doesn't seem to notice as the dog blasts past him and hurls itself at my leg. I scoop him up, laughing as he launches a lick attack to my face. "What kind of ferret dog is this?"

Tam releases me. "Ferret is the fucking word. I have no idea what he is."

"What's his name?"

"Rudolf."

"Rudolf?"

Tam shucks his coat, hoodie, and boots, revealing his tattooed arms, and the fibreglass cast on his wrist. It's green—he let the nurse applying it choose the colour and she'd told him it was Christmassy. At the time, he hadn't seemed to care much, but the shade suits his warm eyes and the dark hair he shakes out. "I found him last December and I was drunk enough that I forgot I'd have to call him that all year round. He's Rudy these days, but it was a hell of a hangover for a while."

"Sounds it. If it's any consolation, the only things I ever find when I'm drunk is bad sex and soggy chips."

"Maybe you're doing it wrong."

"Which part? The sex?"

Tam smirks. "Doubt it."

"Why's that?"

He takes a breath. Then snaps his mouth shut, amusement and something else dancing in his gaze. Something I can't quantify while I'm holding his wriggly dog and trying to ignore the fact I'm flirting with my landlord.

The dog. Talk about the dog. "Where did you find him?"

It's the out Tam needs. He comes closer and tickles Rudy's chin. "Round the back of the dodgy pub in town. He was about to get chucked in the ring as a bait dog."

Horror tosses my stomach. I'm not hungry anymore. "How did you save him?"

"Punched someone. Probably." Tam gives me a shadowed grin. "Can't really remember. Just that I woke up with sore knuckles and a fun-sized tyrant living in my house."

Rudy squirms to get down. I release him and face Tam again. "That's a bit different to finding a stray dog on your way home."

"Is what it is." Tam gestures for me to take off my coat. "And I can't complain. He's the biggest little prick I've ever known, but I love him."

Ugh. Can he get any hotter? I relinquish my coat and leave my shoes on the rustic wood floor of the hallway. It's warm beneath my feet and that warmth continues throughout the ground floor of the house as I follow him into his living space.

The cosy aesthetic isn't a world away from the annex, but it's bigger, and Tam's scent is strong enough that I want to sniff the air and saturate myself in it.

I settle for padding past his couch and trailing him into the open plan kitchen, where he's already at the fridge, pulling out a casserole pot. "What's that?"

He wraps his deep voice around some French words and I just about die.

Also, I have no idea what he said.

"Chicken," he translates. "With lardons and cream. I was going to eat it on the couch with a spoon, but I have pastry too."

Okay. So the answer to my earlier question is a resounding *yes*. Apparently Tam Dubois gets hotter by the second. A tattooed, dog-rescuing man who can cook. Like, did Mother Nature reach into my head and pluck out my wildest fantasies? It's the only explanation I can think of.

And he's not done. Inexplicably, there's more to come.

Tam cuts pastry into a wide circle and chucks it in the oven with his pot of chicken. Then he points to the stairs. "My studio's in the spare room. You want to see?"

He has flour on his hands—even the casted one. At this point, I'm leaning in the doorway for support, and my voice, when I find it, is faint. *Breathless*. "Sure."

"Let me light the fire and I'll show you."

I swear to god, if he starts chopping wood, I'm done. I'm dust on the floor. Sweep me up and chuck me in the wind. But thankfully, Tam makes short work of stuffing logs in the burner and lighting it before...

Leading me upstairs.

To his studio where he makes art out of words with ink, paint, and parchment paper. "You're a...what's the word?"

"Calligrapher," Tam supplies. "Did you think I was a plumber or something?"

Honestly, I'm not sure what I thought. But it wasn't this. I peer at the work he has scattered around. The ink bottles, the pen nibs, and sheets of thick paper. "You have big hands."

Tam laughs. "Okay."

"That's not what I meant."

"I know."

"How?"

"How what?"

I tear my gaze from a Christmas tree comprised of elegant script. "How do you know what I meant?"

"Because no one can ever get their head around me doing something like this. If I'd asked you to imagine a calligrapher ten minutes ago, would you have pictured me?"

I've pictured him in my dreams, I'm sure of it. But he has a point. I don't know what a stereotypical calligrapher looks like, but I'm willing to bet it isn't a six-foot beefcake with skulls tattooed on his knuckles. "All right," I concede. "I might've made an assumption about you based on your appearance. Can't lie, you look like a biker."

The teasing glint in Tam's gaze fades. "I was once."

That gets my attention—as if he didn't already have it. Skylar has lots of biker friends who dress like Tam. Men most people would cross the road to avoid, but I happen to know are some of the nicest people on earth, once you get past the gangster vibe. "What happened to change that? I mean, if you want to share. It's okay if you don't."

I shift my focus to a sheet of recycled cardboard with Christmas greetings etched on it in chalk-white ink. It's gorgeous in its simplicity and so very Tam that I can't believe I didn't see this in him. That I *saw* ink staining his hands and took him for a carpenter. "How do you get the letters like that? I can barely write my own name."

For a long moment, Tam is still—too still. He's marble in whatever dark place my nosiness has forced him back to. Then I feel him move and he fills the space beside me. "You write like a drunk doctor."

"It's way worse than that, trust me. I get told all the time."

"By who?"

"Colleagues, bosses. My mum when I send her postcards."

"Postcards?"

"My parents live in Tasmania."

Tam frowns, placing it. "Australia?"

"They emigrated when I joined the Navy." It's his turn to be surprised—I see it in his high brows and widened gaze. "What? I don't look a military man?"

"It's not that." Tam rotates a little. It brings him so close we're almost touching, shoulder-to-shoulder, thigh-to-thigh. "I just see you more as a healer than a fighter."

"Well, you're right. I was a critical care nurse in the Navy too, and it's a non-combatant role. I was never deployed to a conflict. All my overseas tours were on hospital ships managing natural disasters."

"No guns for you?"

"It's not as cut and dry as that, but no. Shooting people wasn't my main occupation." Tam's nearness starts to dizzy me. I put a little distance between us and study a piece of work that seems more complex than the rest. "What's this?"

"Bible shit."

Looking closer, I can see that. "What's it for?"

"The big church near the hospital in the city. They have me write out their Christmas lesson every year, then I let them mass-produce it as greeting cards to sell in their shop to help fund their food bank."

"That's nice."

"I'm more grateful than nice." Tam's gaze hazes again. "My

brother went off the rails about ten years ago. They helped him get his life back on track when he wouldn't let me anywhere near him."

"The brother you hung up on last week?"

"Sab? Yeah. These days he's *on* the rails so damn hard he makes me look bad."

I doubt anything could make Tam look bad, and I'm enchanted by the piece he's done for the church. The religious words mean nothing to me, but the intricacy of each letter is mesmerising. "How long does something like this take?"

Tam narrows the gap between us and glances over my shoulder. "Couple of days, but you see these smaller cards? I can rattle loads of them out if I get in the zone and nothing distracts me."

I wonder if I'm distracting him. If he's supposed to be working right now instead of being the master of the savoury aroma coming from downstairs. What I'd do if I asked him and he said yes. Because leaving feels impossible and I'm as sucked into his vortex as I was the first night I laid eyes on him. "How did you get into this?"

Tam takes a breath slow enough to make me glance at him. His expression hasn't changed, but the shift in him is hard to miss. "It was therapy, and I turned out to be good at it, so I carried on, and here I am."

Here he is, so close to me again that it takes every ounce of restraint not to lean in and just *feel* him. Brace my weight against his, that rangy warmth, that strength. I want to sniff his neck too, so much it alarms me, but I can't make myself move, except to skim my hand down his un-casted forearm. "Every cloud, eh?"

Tam hums, low and deep, not agreeing or disagreeing. I

want to say more—I *need* to say more, but the oven timer beeps and the moment breaks.

We go downstairs. Tam sits me on a stool and finishes dinner, and that feeling of perfection returns.

"I haven't had a vol-au-vent since the nineties and I'm pretty sure it was tiny and came from the back of my nan's freezer."

Tam laughs and dumps the tray with the giant pastry case on the counter. It's oozing with creamy chicken and bacon and smells almost as edible as he does. "I can cook six things. This is one of them."

"What are the other five?"

He speaks French again.

I nod like I have a clue what he's saying, and he laughs some more.

"I'll show you number two next time you come over."

Next time. I try not to let my grin split my face, and I get lucky as Tam turns away to find plates and cutlery. *Really* lucky as I get to watch him stretch and reach over his head, lifting his shirt enough that I get a glimpse at more tattooed skin and...

The tail end of a brutal scar.

My mouth dries up. I reach for the beer he put in front of me when we came downstairs. French beer, obviously, but it tastes like ash as I swig it and try not to join the dots in my racing mind.

Ex-biker.

Therapy.

Scars.

It doesn't take a genius to deduce that at some point before I met Tam, something terrible happened to him.

"Earth to Bhodi?" Tam waves a hand in front of my face. "Still with me?"

I force a smile. "Where else would I be?"

"Anywhere you want."

I want to be here. But Tam doesn't seem to be the kind of bloke who needs that reassurance. He lets me get my bearings in my own time and flicks on the radio, letting cheesy Christmas music fill the silence. Slade, of course, growling out the tune I've already heard a thousand times in the hospital lifts and it's still November.

"Eat up, son."

Tam slides a plate in front of me. He's added bread. And a salad of green leaves and walnuts I hadn't noticed him pulling together.

"Wow." I reach for the cutlery. "This is the best dinner I've seen in months—probably years."

"What do you usually eat?"

My answer is delayed by me stuffing my face with food as amazing as it looks. "Fuck me, that's good."

Tam slides his fork out of his mouth, lips twitching. "How do you make everything sound like sex?"

"It's a skill. An unintentional one."

"I like it."

"Yeah?"

Tam makes a low sound and reaches for his beer. "Don't encourage me."

He grins a little, but the quip feels loaded in a way I'm not prepared for. That maybe he's not either. So I rewind and answer his question. "I eat terrible things when I'm at work. I try to put it right on my rest days, but I've had a lot going on recently."

A yawn punctuates my words. I eat more, feeling the comforting benefits of real food swamp my system, and I know if I let myself, I could sleep right here with my head on Tam's kitchen counter.

"Do you cook?"

"Me?" I chew a mouthful of salad and nuts, appreciating a combination I'd never have thought of. "Yeah...I mean, I can. Doesn't mean I do. The dude I was seeing—eating wasn't really his thing, and I can't be arsed much when I'm on my own."

It's more than I mean to say, but Tam takes it all in. He asks me more questions and I tell him no lies. We clear our plates, drink beer, and wash up. I learn that his parents live in the south of France, where they moved after he grew up in Solihull, and that his brother—Sab—has a baby girl who Tam adores.

In turn I tell him more about serving overseas, the good, the bad, and the ugly. I don't mind sharing, and I'm greedy for every nugget he gives up about himself in return. But he doesn't say any more about his biker past, the scar on his back, or what unnerves him about the hospital, and midnight rolls around before I know what's happening.

Tam walks me to the door. He has sugar on his lips from the Mr Kipling stash he broke out after the washing up, but he licks it off with a swipe of his tongue too fast for me to fall into thinking about doing it for him.

But I think about it anyway, as we say goodnight and I walk away, and I imagine his gaze on me as I round the fence he repaired a few days ago and let myself into the annex. Then I find myself annoyed that the small space smells of me instead of him. Of the pine-scented detergent I washed my bedsheets in when I couldn't wind down after working all night.

Yesterday, I liked it. I hate it now, and the cosy space feels cold, reminding me that I need to google how to use a log-burner without setting the place on fire, and hang out at home long enough to appreciate my efforts.

I *need* to go shopping.

But thanks to Tam, that can wait, and I swap my clothes for soft joggers and flop onto my bed, letting my thoughts drift and spin until they inevitably return to him. To his dark hair and simmering gaze potent enough to keep the death I brought home from work locked up where it belongs. His concentration as he'd cooked like a boss. The faint shyness when he'd shown me his work, and the gentle flirtation he'd tossed my way all night as if he had no idea how healing it was to the wound Skylar's indifference left behind—a wound that reopens as I lie alone in bed without the balm of Tam's easy company, the gaping hole in my self-esteem widening as insecurities creep in, egged on by the nasty git living on my shoulder.

He wasn't flirting.

Course he wasn't. Why would he? I'm the calamity neighbour who can't get it together enough to cook a meal or fix my own car. He invited me in because I'm pathetic and perhaps I wear my craving for affection all over my stupid face.

Stop.

I try, but I'm not good at regulating negative thoughts when I'm this tired and my brain is searching for something—anything—to avoid processing the work-related disquiet Tam distracted me from with his sexy tats and French cooking. Before Skylar, I'd have picked up my phone and found a hookup. But it's been months since I had anything but my hand for company, and I'm not in the mood for the comedown of a lonely wank.

So, even though I know—I *know*—it's a bad idea, I think

about Tam some more. About his unshaven jaw and olive skin. His rough, tattooed hands that somehow produce the most delicate written art I've ever seen. And the boyish grin he'd dazzled me with as he'd dumped a box of apple pies on the kitchen counter.

"I have a sweet tooth."

Shouldn't be sexy. It is, though, and I feel that reality creep through me, warming my blood and pooling south in my groin.

My dick hardens. It's a reflex to reach for it—to palm myself through my sweats before my hand dips lower. It's masochism to stop myself and groan at the ceiling. Denying myself release is a bad idea, which leads to bad decisions. To *reckless* decisions when I've made a vow to be kinder to my soft heart.

Fuck it.

I give in and wrap my fist around my cock, arching into the sensation even though there's a bruised part of me that wants it over with. My eyes fall shut and I fixate on the slow build of friction and pleasure, jaw clenched, muscles contracting. I know how to make this fast. How to white out my mind with a quickening pace, losing myself in detached ecstasy.

Tonight, though, the harder I chase it, the more out of reach it feels.

Come.

Get it done and go to sleep.

But my dick doesn't get the memo and a frustrated grunt snarls in my throat, neck straining as I grit my teeth, desperate for a blank release, all the while a deeper part of me knows it's not enough. That even if I make it to the end, the gnarly itch in my belly will still be there.

An image invades my brain, unbidden and beautiful. I'm so bowled over by it that it takes me a moment to recognise Tam and his tattooed skin, ink staining his fingers as I pin his wrists over his head and steal a harsh kiss from his lips.

He tastes of sugar and cinnamon. He groans, and it's the spark to the fire that I need. To shove me to that peak as a powerful release steams through me.

Wow. I draw it out a little, blinking through stunned and laboured breaths, as two things occur to me in rapid succession. One, that I'm pretty sure my Tam-themed fantasy was about to take me somewhere I rarely go with men. Two, it didn't get that far because the mere thought of kissing him catapulted me off the edge.

I don't know what to make of it, so I try not to make anything of it at all. I clean up and crawl back into bed, my heart still pounding like a runaway train. I like sex. When I'm not caught in my feelings, it's freeing, and I don't have many boundaries or hang-ups. But it's been a while since I've come that hard, since an orgasm left me shaking, and it sends my mind into a spin all over again.

Idiot. Since when did knocking one out over someone dull their appeal?

Some time around never, and I roll onto my belly with a tortured groan, screwing my eyes shut as the fantasy I've just come to threatens to boil over again, tempered only by the kind of emotional flagellation that leaves scars on your soul.

You think he's lying awake with you on his mind?

It feels as likely as the notion that Tam was flirting with me earlier, and it's enough to smother the fire my misguided self-love has stoked in my blood.

Tam's not thinking about me, so I need to stop thinking about him. Tam Dubois. My *landlord* and a man I've known for less than two weeks and I'm already—

Nope.

Not doing it.

I force myself to sleep and wake up with an iron curtain around my mind.

Get up.

Run.

Eat.

Find a new hobby.

Great advice and I heed every scrap of it, until I exit the annex in my long-neglected workout clothes to find a bag of groceries on the doorstep, complete with a work-of-art note that melts the barrier I've imagined into a puddle at my feet.

Bhodi Jones,

You need to eat. Don't let life stop you.

Tam x

Seven

TAM

I'm dead.

I thought it would wear off, the wild feeling in my chest every time I'm near Bhodi. Then I accidentally caught a glimpse of him lying half naked in bed with his cock in his fist and everything I'd put down to the temporary thrill of making a new friend, who just so happens to be hotter than sin, solidified. Put down roots. *Cemented* that shit in my brain.

He's not something I think about anymore.

He's *all* I think about, and it's freaking me out.

"Merde, you have it bad." Sab gets in my face, literally. For the first time in a while, we're not bickering through a phone screen. He's in my garden, inspecting my work on the fence under the pretence that he's not trying to catch a glimpse of Bhodi. "How hot is this lodger, exactly?"

"Hot enough." I speak from the back door. It's raining and if there's one thing I hate more than being cold, it's being wet and cold. Also, Bhodi's not even home. I just like watching Sab waste his time.

He eventually runs out of fence to pick fault with and sidles back to where I'm slouching, nursing the same tea I've been carrying around all morning, too distracted to fucking drink it. "Are you going to hook up with him?"

"What? No. Course I'm not. He's my tenant."

"So?"

"So, that's fucked up."

"Why? Sounds like porn to me."

I feint an elbow to Sab's ribs.

He laughs. "What's wrong with that? It's what you like, isn't it? Kinky sex with no strings?"

"No *complications.*"

"And..."

"Fucking my tenant would be complicated."

"Depends how you do it, mon frère. Surely your repertoire isn't that basic?"

I jab him for real. He rolls with the blow and ambles inside to raid my fridge.

Scowling, I follow and try not to fixate on the front gate, where I last saw Bhodi as he jogged past with bed head and black running sweats, a feat that only leads me back in time, to the evening he spent in my kitchen, eating dinner and making me laugh more than I have in years.

To what happened next.

I saw him.

Back arched, skin flushed. Bottom lip caught between his teeth. His dick—

"How's work?"

"What?"

Sab smirks from the fridge door, letting me know I was an absolute fucking idiot to tell him even the briefest version of what happened a few nights ago. "I was right the first time."

"About what?"

"About you having it bad for the lodger."

"He has a name."

Sab clutches his chest. "Stop. Mon cœur!"

"You fucking stop."

He does for as long as it takes him to hoover up every scrap of bread and ham in my kitchen. Then he's on me again because he cares as much as he loves to watch me squirm.

"How much dick did you actually see?"

Sab's even messier than me. I sweep crumbs from the counter and consider thumping him again, but it's hard to think about violence when his question fills my head with... other things. Also, without the safety net of a phone screen, bullshitting my brother is impossible. It's easier to tell him the truth and worry about what he'll do with it later. "I saw enough."

"It was a good one?"

"The whole package was good, but I knew that already."

"How?"

A sigh breaches my lungs. "Putain de bordel de merde. I have to explain this to you again?"

"Fucking right, you do." Sab hops onto the counter, still stuffing his face with stolen food. "You keep telling me you just want casual dick or whatever. Then you start seeing someone and it's all about the bigger picture. Make it make sense."

"I'm not seeing Bhodi."

"That's the shittest answer I've ever heard."

"Then go ask someone else how attraction works. I don't know what to tell you."

I have a shit-ton of work to do. I leave Sab and Rudy to entertain each other, and stomp upstairs to the studio with every intention of making the most of what's left of the daylight. But of course my gaze drifts to the annex and Bhodi's bed. It's empty, but I see him there all the same, and this time I'm not thinking about his dick, or if he came as hard as I did in the shower two minutes after I ripped myself away from the window. I'm thinking about how he looks when he sleeps. When he laughs. When he leaned back in his seat that night and rubbed his stomach, smiling at me like I'd hung the moon when all I'd done was share my dinner with him.

That's it.

That's the fucking package. I didn't need to see Bhodi's dick to know he's sexy as fuck.

Now, I just need to stop thinking about it.

Working eats up the rest of my day. I get ahead on the bigger projects, but fall behind on the billion greetings card orders that have come in thick and fast over the past week. Pretty sure Sab knocks out on the couch. Either way, it's the evening by the time he shuffles upstairs to say goodbye.

"Stay," I offer, even though I'm done with his nonsense for one day. "You've missed Esme's bedtime already and you're working in Worcester tomorrow."

Sab stands from lacing his boots, lines from the couch cushions imprinted on his face. "Not worth the grief."

"What isn't? Spending the night with me or telling Charmaine you're not coming home?"

"All of it." He heads for the door. "Thanks, though."

I follow him out, forgetting my shoes and cursing as my

socks get wet from the rain-soaked path. "Did you really come all the way down here to take a nap?"

"What do you think?"

"I think you're an idiot for driving three hours home, only to turn around and come back again in the morning." At five a.m., when even if he leaves right now, he's not going to reach his front door till gone eleven.

But despite Sab being the reigning king of unsolicited advice, he doesn't care for being on the receiving end. He leaves in a huff of irritation, only to call me before I get a wet foot inside.

"Sorry. You know I love you."

I do. And I know why he's telling me. We've learned the hard way not to say goodbye on an argument and I know it haunts Sab more than it haunts me. I put him on speaker while I stop Rudy streaking down the garden for no reason that doesn't mean more wet mud in my house. "I love you too. That's why I wanted you to stay. So you're not driving that van through exhaustion in the morning."

"Bro, I have a baby. I haven't slept since she was born."

"Exactly. You're already fucking knackered."

"Tam, I'm fine. I promise."

My brother rarely says my name. Or keeps his decorum long enough to have a real conversation. Humour is his armour against the world. And perhaps it's mine too. The world feels fucked up if Sab's not laughing at me. "What's wrong?"

"Nothing."

"Liar."

He grunts. "Says you."

"What's that supposed to mean?"

"It means you're being weird about the hot lodger. I thought you were getting over what happened with Grey."

"I haven't been with Grey for six fucking years."

"Exactly!" I hear Sab's fist connect with the steering wheel. Of the two of us, he's the most dramatic when he's pissed off. He shouts and thumps things.

Me? I fester. Stubborn, remember? Why fix something with a five-second tantrum when you can stew on it for a lifetime? "I'm not hung up on Grey."

Sab says nothing, which is as dangerous as it is uncharacteristic.

"Or the hot lodger."

Sab snorts, the barest hint of a laugh. Then he sighs, still serious enough for me to forget I'm standing on my wet doorstep with no shoes on. "Je m'inquiète pour toi. I know you've been through a lot, but don't you think it's time you made room for something more than empty fucks that never go anywhere?"

He's had all day to say this shit. Now he's doing it as he drives away from me. It's very us—very *me*, and guilt pinches my heart, even though I know Sab well enough to suspect being concerned for my love life isn't the only thing winding him up. "If it's any consolation, I had dinner with Bhodi before I saw his dick through the window."

"You did what?"

"I had food. He was hungry. I shared it."

I leave out the part about dragging Bhodi into my house without asking him if he wanted to come in. Or how right it felt that he didn't protest and stayed all evening, and that I woke at the crack of dawn to sneak a bag of groceries onto his doorstep.

But what I do share is enough to bemuse Sab enough that he's lost for words again.

Mostly, anyway. "You had date night and sent him home to have a wank by himself. That's a zero-star rating on your personality."

"It wasn't date night, you fuckwit. How many times do I have to tell you I'm never hooking up with my tenant?"

"You can tell me as much as you like, doesn't mean you won't hook up with him."

I grab the phone and detonate in a flurry of French curses that have Sab laughing and hanging up on me before I'm done. The fucker. I mean, I'll take it if it means he's driving home with a smile on his face, but I could still reach through the phone and throttle him.

"That sounded lairy."

I spin around. Bhodi's by the gate, resting his elbows on it as if he's been there all night. Or for the entirety of a conversation that should've happened in my house with the door shut.

Fuck. I scrutinise him for signs of offence, but I find nothing but his easy smile, and the fact he's not wearing gym gear anymore. He's in jeans that hang from his trim hips and a faded Vans tee hiding his chest from me.

He came home and I didn't notice.

It should feel like progress.

It doesn't.

"My brother." I test the waters. "He likes winding me up to deflect from his own shit."

A beat passes. Then Bhodi grins. "You could tell me you were proposing marriage to Father Christmas and I'd believe you. I don't speak French."

Relief washes over me. "You're not missing much when it comes to conversing with my brother. He's a pain in the arse."

"But you love him."

"How can you tell?"

"You're smiling."

"Not on purpose." Unbidden, my gaze sweeps him again. "Where's your coat?"

"Where are your shoes?"

He has me there, but in the short space of time I've known Bhodi, he hasn't ventured out of the annex for any reason other than to leave the property, and he doesn't look like he's going anywhere right now.

I feel drawn to him, and I let it happen, my wet socks squelching on the puddled steps as I join him at the gate. "What are you doing out here in the rain?"

Bhodi's smile shifts to one that's almost shy. "I was making dinner for the first time in a hundred years and I was going to ask if you wanted some."

"You were *going to* ask?"

"I got distracted by you growling in French."

"It put you off?"

Bhodi chuckles. "Not exactly. But I still have a giant pot of bolognese and you look hangry, so..."

I'm not anywhere close to being angry while he's so close to me that I can smell the shampoo he used on his damp hair. But I am hungry, and Sab ate all my food. *And*...I like being around Bhodi. The ease. The laughter. It's so natural to say yes. To change my socks, grab Rudy, and follow my tenant back to the annex he pays me to live in.

I step into the space that until a month ago, had been my studio for half a decade. It should smell of paper and ink. But instead, the rich scent of tomatoes and herbs greets me, along with the bed Bhodi sleeps on, a neat pile of clean clothes, and the mega-watt smile he turns on me from the tiny kitchen area.

It's a two-ring hob I installed to make tea on—because I hate electric kettles. A sink, two cupboards, and a narrow length of worktop made out of the same oak that crushed my wrist. I'm impressed Bhodi's found the space to cook something that smells this good.

I tell him so.

He laughs.

I die a little in the very best way.

"We eat spag bol at Christmas in my family. I'm working this year, but I said I'd bring some to the ward to make up for them having to translate my notes. This is a practise run."

There's a lot to unpick in that. I start with what disturbs me most. "You eat spaghetti at Christmas? Are you Italian?"

Bhodi peers into the simmering pot before he gifts me that laugh again. "Definitely not Italian. It's more it's the only thing my mum can cook that everyone likes, so...it's what we have, for three days, until everyone goes back to work."

"Sounds like your family are busy people."

"Used to be. It's only me who works shifts these days."

"And your parents are in Australia now, right?"

"Right." Bhodi finds plates and looks around for somewhere to put them.

There isn't anywhere. I converted this place for work, not hot dinner dates.

Not a date.

I take the plates, balancing them on my good hand so Bhodi can dish up. "Do you miss them?"

"Who? My parents?" Bhodi adds pasta to the plates—it's

not even spaghetti, which perplexes me more—and spoons on the meat sauce. "Not really. I haven't lived with them since I was sixteen, and we've never been close. They both worked a lot."

"Is that why you left?"

"When I was sixteen? Nah, I just hated school, so I ran off to join the Navy."

I know this part. That he served and he doesn't smile so much when I push him on it. So I don't. I hold the plates and try to figure out where we can sit to eat.

Rudy's already made himself a nest in Bhodi's clean clothes. "Sorry about that. His blanket used to be over there."

Bhodi moves around me and collapses the sofa-bed, tucking the duvet away behind it. "You used to live in here?"

"It was my studio."

"For real?" Bhodi glances around, clearly comparing the space to the smaller room I'm holed up in now. "Please tell me I didn't push you out of here?"

"*I* pushed me out of here—well, Sab did. There's not a lot of money in calligraphy these days, outside of the occasional unicorn job."

"What does a unicorn job look like?"

"I did the official invites for the royal carol concert last year."

"Right here? In this room?"

I set the plates I'm still holding on the coffee table and tug Bhodi a little to the left where my desk used to be. "Right *here*."

He's not expecting my touch. It wavers his balance, toppling him into me, and of course we notice in the same moment. "Um..."

An awkward chuckle escapes me. "Um. Yeah. Anyway. I used to work in here, now I don't. But it's not your fault AI and digital art make it tough for me to earn a living. I like a challenge."

"That right?" Bhodi skewers me with a hot glance before he reins it in and steps away. "Damn. Sorry."

"What for?"

Bhodi gestures for me to take a seat on the folded sofa-bed. "For getting in your face all the time. I don't mean to, it just falls out of me when I'm around you."

I should be relieved that it's happening to him too. That it isn't just me who turns into an idiot when we're together. But I don't think about that. It barely crosses my mind. Instead I let myself ask the real question. The reckless one that's going to make this a hundred times worse. "What makes you think I don't like you flirting with me?"

"A few things." Bhodi pokes at his dinner, not eating, his gaze distant for a loaded second. "Before today, I wasn't sure you were even into dudes. Then...I kinda did hear some of what you and your brother said earlier, and I got the impression that my brand of fuck-awful flirting is the last thing you want right now."

"That's what you heard?"

Bhodi nods, his jewel-bright gaze free of bullshit, and this time, the relief makes land. I mean, this isn't great, but it's better than him overhearing me talk about his dick.

His *gorgeous* dick.

"Sab worries about me. He told me a while ago that I'm going to die alone."

Bhodi flinches. "That's not nice."

"He didn't mean it—he just worries about me."

"Because you've been through a lot?"

"You heard that too?"

"I think so. A lot of it really was in French and I backed up a bit when I realised you were fighting."

"We weren't fighting."

Bhodi eats, disagreeing without words. But if he thinks what he saw tonight was the height of a Dubois throwdown, he's in for a shock if he sticks around.

He's not sticking around. It's a six-month tenancy.

I kill that thought and dig into the dinner someone else has cooked for me. And it's so fucking good for reasons beyond that it tastes amazing. "I can't remember the last time someone cooked me dinner."

"Sab doesn't cook for you?"

"Not as much as he should. He's like a fridge-raiding hamster these days."

"It's nice that you're close." Bhodi finishes up and sets his plate aside. "I miss having someone around who gives a shit what happens to me."

I get the feeling he's not talking about his family, and my curiosity must show on my face.

Bhodi sighs and scrubs a hand down his face. "I don't want to bring up my ex every time I see you."

I nudge him with my foot. "Doesn't mean you can't."

"It should. He's not even my ex."

I swallow the last of my dinner, forcing it down. "No?"

It shouldn't shock me that Bhodi has unfinished business with someone. He's beautiful. Funny. Nice. I can't imagine anyone walking away from him and not coming back to rectify their mistake.

"We were never really together," Bhodi clarifies, which somehow feels worse. "It was a hookup that got under my skin.

I started to care about him too much, while he really was just fucking me."

"Did you love him?"

I don't mean to say it, but the words spill out of my mouth and I can't take them back any more than I can kid myself that I'm not hanging on his answer more than I have any right to be. That it doesn't twist me up that thinking about this other dude tightens Bhodi's jaw and reddens his eyes.

"I tried really hard not to," he says eventually. "And he never did anything to lead me on. It was just really...difficult to be with someone who *needed* to be loved so much, and not give in to it. Probably doesn't make much sense..."

"It does."

"Really?"

I'm distracted for a moment by Rudy abandoning Bhodi's clean clothes in favour of investigating the plates on the coffee table, but he's shit out of luck. Little bastard's too short.

I tell him so and shoo him away. Then I'm back in Bhodi's vortex and it feels good, even though I hate the sadness in his eyes. "I was with a dude once who was hardcore in love with someone else. I thought that suited me—no attachments, complications, whatever. Just sex. But it still wound up hurting to know he was thinking of another bloke the whole time."

"The *whole* time?"

I shrug. "Maybe not. We had some mad sex. But I always knew I was keeping him warm for someone better, and in the end, I wasn't as okay with it as I thought I'd be."

Bhodi's fair brows are still raised to his hairline. "Someone better?"

"Better *for him*," I amend.

"Did you want something more?"

"No."

"Not even a little bit?"

"Caring about someone doesn't mean you want to be with them. I liked his company, and I loved the kinky sex he was into. There were probably moments that tied all that together in a pretty Christmas bow, but when I see him now, I don't wish that he found what he has now with me."

Bhodi gets up and takes the plates to the sink. He comes back with a bottle of spiced rum and two glasses he must've brought with him when he moved in. "I'm getting there with Skylar, but I'm trying not to do what I usually do to get over something that's hurt me."

"And what's that?"

"Fuck someone else."

"It might help."

"*Or...*" Bhodi pours rum and passes me one. "It might be time I broke the cycle. I like kinky sex too, but it hasn't got me anywhere."

He likes kinky sex. It's so far from the point he's trying to make, but for a hot second, it's all I hear, and my mind tumbles into the abyss.

How kinky? Exactly?

The word is a spectrum, a fucking wide one, and the craving to know where Bhodi falls on it hits a high and keeps climbing until I get a hold of myself.

I swig rum. The burn grounds me in Christmas-spiced fire. "Sounds like you need more than sex, even if you've got yourself believing you don't want it."

"Isn't that what your brother was trying to say to you?"

"It was." I can't lie. "Doesn't mean he was right, though."

81

Bhodi smiles and necks his own rum. Then pours another. "Doesn't mean he was wrong."

I don't find a retort. Instead I sip rum and settle into the couch I bought off Etsy a month ago believing a nondescript human I'd never have to think about would sleep on it. It still blows my mind that in the short time Bhodi's been my tenant, he's become *all* I think about.

It should unnerve me, like it's clearly unnerved Sab. But it's hard to feel anything but chill as Bhodi mirrors my pose and we settle as close as we had in the fracture clinic's waiting room.

We drink more rum. I get brave and ask Bhodi more about his job.

"Do you work in A&E?"

"No." He swipes rum from his lips with his thumb. "I did HEMS calls for a while when I left the Navy, but I don't enjoy all the blood and guts. I'm better at keeping patients alive once they've been put back together."

"So you work on...?"

"HDU, mainly. It's attached to the intensive care unit."

I know that. I nearly died up there. More than once. But rum and Bhodi help me blast past that and focus on him. "You must still have tough days."

"Lots. But I see some amazing things too. People who walk out smiling when they should've died before I met them. That's the best part of it."

"Do you wear scrubs or one of those fancy tops?"

"Scrubs. They're *green*."

His nose crinkles. Combined with his hair that's dried sticking up, as though I've rolled him around on the rug, it's cute. "You don't like them?"

"I don't like anything green. Except that Christmas tree card you showed me the other day. I liked that."

"Good to know."

"Why?"

Like they have so many times, our gazes lock. I fall into his and he falls into mine. I want to lean closer. To be there waiting, when he does. But I hold back, so does he, and the moment almost passes.

And maybe it would've if he'd been someone else.

If I'd been less transparent to him.

"You know…" Bhodi sets his glass down. "It feels really good to talk about this stuff with someone who understands. Like, it's starting to dawn on me that I need a friend more than I need some banging sex."

"What about shit sex? That might be all I'm good for."

A rum-fuelled laugh spills out of Bhodi. He's not drunk. Neither am I. But the rum has softened the edges on both of us, and there's nothing awkward about this. "I know you're not shit at sex, Tam."

"How?"

He gives me an unsubtle once-over. "It would be the cruellest trick if you were."

That's it. All I'm getting. But it's okay, I know what he's saying. Bhodi's hotter than sin. It defies physics to even contemplate him being a bad fuck. So I contemplate him being a good one—the best—and it gets me in all kinds of trouble with my conscience.

He needs a friend, remember?

I can't forget it. I *want* it. To be the person he stares at like this and gives up his darkest secrets to. His lightest secrets. All of it. So I give him one of mine. "I think I need a friend too."

Bhodi smiles, his eyes twinkling in the moonlight slowly cloaking the room as the rainclouds pass. "There's an obvious solution here. Can't promise I'll never flirt with you, though."

"It's banter if we're friends. Totally doesn't count."

It should. I want to be Bhodi's friend, like my fucking soul knows how much I need it. But none of that dulls the current pinging between us. The impact of every charged comment. Every casual touch that leaves a smouldering burn in its wake.

The droll glance Bhodi sends my way tells me he knows this as well as I do, but he doesn't argue. He *yawns*, and it's catching.

Rudy's already snoring up a storm in the washing he's kicked up into a royal mess.

I rise, stretching, my head a little lighter than when I arrived and it's not all rum.

Bhodi stands too and for a protracted moment we stare before he goes for the hug—a real hug, all warm arms and affection we haven't earned, and yet somehow feels so fucking right it's all I can do not to melt against him.

He smells so good. I take a deep inhale and hold him tighter, soaking up how his hard body feels against mine. How his slightly brawnier bulk fits the leanness that's stayed with me over the past six years. If I let my mind wander, I'll find myself picturing us pressed together in different ways. If I don't let go soon, I'll act on it. But beyond the blaze his embrace stokes in me, there's peace too, as if Bhodi's good heart can heal mine, and I don't let go.

I don't want to.

So I hold on until Bhodi leans back.

And that's when I realise my mistake.

We're wrapped up in each other, our faces inches apart. His hair tickles my cheek and I scent the rum on his lips.

This is bad.

So very bad.

But the trouble with bad things that aren't really bad at all, is that walking away from them takes superhuman strength. Strength I've never had. And in this moment, I don't want strength. I want Bhodi. A taste. A kiss. A soft brush of lips that's rum and mischief, and his quiet laugh as he realises what we're doing, and he doesn't stop.

I don't stop either. I sink into a kiss so fucking sweet I might die from the gentle force of it. And the irony. Because if I've learned anything tonight it's that behind Bhodi's bright eyes and smiley smile, he's probably a filthy bastard.

A filthy *lay*.

Fuck. My hand slides over his hip, hooking him closer in the same moment his warm palm skims up my spine, finding the nape of my neck. The kiss deepens, stealing my breath and what's left of my non-existent willpower. I feel him harden against me and that thrill, that rush of attraction, is so potent it dizzies me.

I want him—

"Damn." Bhodi pulls back. "So this friends thing is going well."

I'm so dazed, I have nothing but a startled laugh.

He laughs too and smooths my rumpled shirt. "Sorry about that."

"Don't be sorry."

"I'm not."

"You lied?"

Bhodi grins. "Yeah."

Man, he's so fucking beautiful that I'm back to staring, transfixed by his wicked gaze and reddened lips. And I need to *go*. Before I forget everything he's said tonight about needing more than whatever hot mess I'm about to lead him into. How I need more than that too.

Rudy.

Like he knows, and maybe he does, my little bastard dog chooses this moment to notice something ridiculous outside. He barks, shrill and *loud*, and it breaks the hot tension stringing me and Bhodi together.

I find my boots and stamp into them while Bhodi watches from a safe distance. He's still smiling, which is good. Me? I'm a mess, but I've spent years pretending I'm not, so I've got this. I muster a grin and plaster it on, and somehow I find the will to leave him and walk out the door.

Eight

BHODI

I kissed my landlord.

 Six seconds after we pledged to be friends.

A mantra that plays on repeat in my head, but as hard as I search for regret, it's not there. It's hard to regret something that blew my mind the way Tam's kiss did. How hot and *right* his body felt against mine. His soft lips and rough palms. With how prone I've been to catching feelings for dudes who make me feel good, it's hard not to be scared to death of it too, but that's a worry for another day. Right now, all I can think about is how he felt in my arms even before I kissed him. How he relaxed into me like he'd been waiting for my embrace his whole life.

And how badly I want to hold him again.

It's a far cry from the casual sex I've spent the last few months convincing myself is all I want out of life, and that's probably the part that terrifies me. But as the rest of the week unfolds and I manage to eat dinner with Tam twice more without laying a hand on him, I begin to calm down.

Friends.

Yeah.

I can do this.

"Is this a five or an S?"

I jump out of my skin, startled out of my Tam-themed daze by my boss bearing down on me, a stack of patient charts clutched in her hands. "Show me?"

Marla dumps the offending chart on the desk, tapping the chicken scratch that's irrefutably mine. "This one."

"It's an S. Why would it be a five?"

"Your writing is terrible."

"I know, but—" Nope. Not doing it. What's the point? Logic doesn't come into it if you can't get the basics right, and I'm the one who can't write a simple sentence without confusing the heck out of people who don't have time to chase me around. "Sorry."

Marla's a tough crowd. She ignores my smile and crosses out my scrawl. "I need you to stay late. Constance has a childcare issue and she needs to go home."

It's already late. Midnight came and went a while ago, bringing with it an influx of patients booted from ICU to make room for the victims of a house fire in the city. HDU is full to bursting. Even without losing a nurse from the night shift, I wasn't expecting to leave any time soon. "It's fine. I need to eat, though."

Understatement. The last real meal I consumed was the potato and ham thing—the *tartiflette*—Tam brought to my door yesterday morning. He didn't hang around to eat it with me, but it was still good enough that I ate the whole thing and fell into a carb coma for the rest of the day before I rocked up here.

Good enough that I daydream about it at any given moment.

Any moment I don't daydream about *him*.

I don't have time for anything but a jaunt to a nearby vending machine. I buy three packets of crisps and a can of Pepsi. Scran it all and get back to work. Marla pulls me up on my paperwork three more times before I finally leave.

It's early morning. Dawn, in fact, a reality that won't be beautiful until I escape the city and reach the pretty little town Tam calls home. That *I* call home—at least for the next few months. But I have to scrape a thick frost from my car—the one that's still running like a dream thanks to Tam's healing hands —before that can happen, and it just about kills me.

I'm tired and I'm hungry, two things that ravage my ability to manage my emotions, and by the time I pull onto Stardust Lane, I'm too frazzled to figure out if I'm happy or sad. Then I see a tall figure headed my way, a tiny dog at his feet, and my mood brightens with the glittery winter sun.

Tam.

I pull up beside him and open the window.

He braces his good arm on the car roof and lets me see his scruffy jaw and dry half smile. "Morning."

"Morning." I kill the engine. "What are you doing up so early?"

"Walking Rudy before the postman's out and about."

"He doesn't like him?"

"Doesn't like anyone, except you and Sab."

"That must be awkward when you have other friends around."

"You see me letting anyone else in my house?"

He must do sometimes. To have the *mad sex* he alluded to the night we kissed. But I let it go. If Tam wants to play lone wolf, who am I to stop him?

"Why are you so late? I thought you were finishing at midnight?"

I've zoned out. I come back to find Tam's dark stare has intensified, and I'm not ready for it.

I deflect by opening the door and stepping out, bringing myself to his level. It's easier to handle being around him when he's not towering over me. For *reasons*. Dirty reasons I'm too tired to contemplate without embarrassing myself. "Busy night."

"Are you okay?"

"Me?"

Tam cocks his head. "There's no one else here, son."

"Rudy's here."

"He's taking a piss up your car."

I shoot a glance down.

Tam laughs. "Made you look."

"Very funny."

"I thought so." Tam twinkles that droll grin at me again. "Are you working tonight?"

"No."

"Good."

"Is it?"

"Bhodi, you're knackered." He states it like the fact it is. "Go to bed. I'll catch up with you later."

"That a promise?" Yeah. Because for all we haven't kissed again, and for all we've sworn to be *friends*, I'm never too tired to flirt with this dude. Or ogle him as he leans into my car to retrieve the keys I've forgotten, shut the window and click the lock before straightening to tuck the keys into my hand.

The whole thing lasts less than thirty seconds, but it does something to me, and I'm smiling by the time he meets my gaze again.

Tam frowns. "What?"

"Nothing. Just delirious."

"Over what?"

You. "Nothing a friend wants to hear about."

"Says who?"

Tam leans closer as he speaks, a shift that's hard to read as subconscious or deliberate.

Either way, it's a struggle to not react. To step back, towards the side gate I need to slip through to reach my bed. "Says *me*. But I have chicken and...something, I was going to cook later if you're interested?"

Tam's frown evaporates, replaced by the subtle lift his whole face gets every time I offer him food. The same contentment I feel every time he cooks for me. "I'm interested."

"All right. Come by about six?"

It's when he stops working. I've noticed this on the evenings I'm at home. How my day is punctuated by Rudy screaming around the garden and Tam growling into his phone at his brother. I try not to listen, and they haven't talked about me since *that* night, but even if I'm dead asleep, I still know Tam's done for the day the second I open my eyes.

We part ways. I don't know where he goes because I don't let myself watch. I traipse myself to the front door of the annex and jam the key in the lock.

I almost trip over the package on the step.

The croissants, cooked ham, and soft-boiled eggs that make

me feel like whoever left them there is the best new friend I could ever make.

I sleep all day. Wish I could say it's restful, but any night worker will tell you it isn't. I'm not awake, but I'm *aware*, and by the time evening rolls around, I feel like I've lived a thousand lives.

The box Tam left me is on the floor by the bed. I hoovered up the food hours ago before I passed out. All that's left is the ornate scrap of paper, decorated with a simple message.

Don't forget about yourself xx

He wrote the words in the shape of a Christmas star. In gold ink on black paper. Can't say why that means something, but I can't stop looking at it, when I'm supposed to be up and at 'em, cooking him dinner.

Shower.

I roll out of bed and into the tiny bathroom. The shower is basic, but runs from the same combi boiler that services the main house. Hot water for days; my old place had a dribble that lasted three and half minutes.

I'm cooked by the time I get out. It takes a second for me to hear the insistent beep of my phone.

It's ringing.

Somewhere.

I search the bed and find it buried under the duvet. It's the time of year where my mum gets emotional and calls more than once a month. I expect her name on the screen. But it's not her.

Skylar.

Confusion throws me. We've barely spoken in months, even before I gave my old job notice and had to work *sixteen* more torturous weeks knowing I could run into him at any moment. But...I don't hate him. Skylar never led me on. He never lied. All he did was walk away when he was done fucking me.

The call rings out.

It's in me to leave it at that, but I'm curious enough to call him back.

He answers quick enough that I know his phone was in his hand. "Hey."

"Hey yourself. Everything all right?"

"So so." I hear the easy smile in Skylar's tone. The one he wears as a shield, when the truth is it hides nothing at all. "How's the new job?"

"Getting there. What do you care?"

"HDU is a mess without you."

"So?"

"Bhodi, I care."

"No, you don't. And that's okay. You don't have to pretend."

Skylar's silent so long I think about regretting my bluntness, all the while pondering how his gravelly Stockport accent doesn't affect me the way used to. But it's a thought that doesn't go anywhere. Being honest with him would've given us both a chance to walk away before I got myself hurt. It's too late for that now, but I'm done kidding myself our relationship is —*was*—something it isn't.

"I'm not pretending to care about you," Skylar says eventually. "I want us to be friends, and I'm really fucking sorry if I've made that impossible by being a cold bastard."

"You're not cold, Skylar."

He isn't. I've worked alongside him enough to know that. But I can't escape the scars his indifference left behind. I don't want to—it's how we learn, right?

"I don't mean to be," Skylar amends. "I never meant to hurt you."

"I know that. It's not your fault I got more into it than you signed up for."

"That's what happened?"

"Technically, you fucked me for three months, then ghosted me on and off for a year, but whatever."

"I'm sorry."

"Why?"

And why *now*?

I picture Skylar lying on the couch in the A&E break room with his phone on his chest, but the more distance I have from him the more I realise I never knew him at all. Not really. A few bunk-ups after work isn't enough for that. We never ate together. Drank together. We never talked like this, because he didn't want to. Not with me. And it's getting easier not to take that personally. I'm not too churned up to know something's happened in his life to make him the way he is. It's not that *I* don't care. I do. But I'm not his person for this shit.

I never was.

We talk a little while longer, about work, mainly. Skylar never answers my question. Then he's gone again, but I don't feel empty without him. I feel like maybe we can be friends.

A knock at the door breaks me from my thoughts.

Tam.

It has to be. No one else can reach the annex without a gate key or going through his house. And *he's* the one I count as my friend.

Maybe that's why I forget I just got out of the shower and open the door in nothing but a towel. Doesn't explain Tam's hot gaze and raised brows, but here we are.

"You're naked," he states.

"Not quite. Give me a second."

I wave him in and duck into the bathroom with some clean clothes.

Dressed, I return to find him exactly where I left him, smirk still in place. "I never said it was a bad thing."

"Doesn't mean it's a good thing. Are you coming in or staying out there all night?"

Tam eyes me as he winces. "I really fucking want to, even though you put your clothes on, but I have a ton of deliveries to make that I forgot about and I won't be back till later. You didn't cook already, did you?"

"Uh. *No.* Not even close. I took a shower and got waylaid by the past."

"Your ex?"

"He's not my ex, but how did you know?"

Tam props a shoulder on the doorframe. "You look like your brain just got turned inside out."

"What does that look like?"

He straightens and steps over the threshold of the annex in one fluid movement. There's a mirror on the hallway wall. Tam guides me in front of it and nudges my mouth with his finger and thumb, coaxing my lips into a smile. "That's better. Now tell me who I need to punch."

"You're ridiculous."

"I'm your *friend.*" Though the way he easily fills the space behind me is anything but friendly. "Someone upsets you, I want them dead. That's how this works."

"I've never had a friend willing to commit murder on my behalf."

"Then you've never had a friend like me."

That, I can believe. But I don't want him hating on Skylar. "No one upset me. He called. We talked. About nothing, but everything's cool."

"*You're* cool." Tam lets his hand drop. If we were lovers, he might've kissed my neck. But he steps back with a rueful sigh. "And I hear you. I saw an old fuck buddy a few weeks before you moved in. I haven't been with him in years and we were never together, but it still affects me to see him."

"You wish things were different?"

"No, that's not it. River's madly in love with the person he was always meant to be with and I love to see it."

"Then what makes you sad when you see him?"

"I never said I felt sad."

"Okay."

Tam rolls his eyes, but I see his concession all the same and I understand more than I want to. I *feel* that pit of loneliness in his gut that he's scared to acknowledge. The one he buries with casual sex and the pretence it's all he'll ever want.

It's the same self-inflicted fallacy I came here with, but I'm not as rooted in it as Tam seems to be, and the big fat lie I'm telling myself is harder to believe.

It'll get easier. Though, the only thing that feels easy right now is breathing Tam's cinnamon scent and leaning way too close to our newly established friendship boundaries. "Don't worry about dinner. I can leave some for you, or we can have it tomorrow, maybe?"

Tam twitches, as if he wants to touch me too. "I've got a better idea. Come with me?"

Nine

TAM

Dragging Bhodi around the city doesn't feel good. But the deliveries I make there don't take long, and then I drive back into town and park behind a church so vast and grand it's more like a cathedral.

He's quiet, taking it all in, not even commenting on the clumsy way I'm gripping the gearstick with my casted hand. If we'd spent the short time we'd known each other exchanging pleasantries on the driveway, I probably wouldn't notice. But we've shared more than that, and I hate the distant haze in his eyes enough to poke him. "Still with me?"

Bhodi tears his gaze from the church to meet mine. "Hmm?"

"Just checking you're awake."

"I'm awake."

He smiles to prove it and it drowns me in all the best things, but I'm not done working yet, and we're *friends*. I can't pinch his cheeks and claim his mouth. So I get out of the van instead and grab the last box I need to deliver tonight.

It's small, but Bhodi pops up at my side anyway. "Need a hand?"

"Got two, thanks."

"Sure about that?" He eyeballs my good hand—the one that aches like a motherfucker from overuse. "You'll be down to none if you're not careful."

I give him the same look he gave me when I knew without him having to tell me that his ex had ruined his day. "How did you pick up on that when you've had your eyes closed since we left Hereford?"

"One, my eyes weren't closed. Two, you've been flexing it since you knocked on my door."

I tuck the box under my arm and make a fist, gritting my teeth against the strain in the weary tendons. "I don't usually write so much with this one. It's better at painting."

His eyes widen. "You really are ambidextrous?"

"Yup."

"Wow." Bhodi reaches for my hand. Second guesses himself. Then does it anyway. "That's super rare. Where does it hurt?"

I show him. He switches to nurse mode so fast I barely catch it, but damn if it isn't sexy as hell.

"Can I try something?"

I lick my dry lips. "Sure."

Bhodi presses my palm. Hard. Then he smooths it over my thumb joint and the relief that rocks me is so damn good I have to lean on the van to stay upright. "Fucking hell."

He smiles, but for once it's faint, his lovely face a study in concentration as he repeats the motion over and over, chasing every ounce of pain from my hand with his magic thumb. "Better?"

"Are you taking the piss?"

"No. It's a real question."

I struggle for words, at least ones that aren't me begging him to touch every part of me with his healing fucking hands. "It's better."

"What about the other one?"

"It's fine. Enjoying the holiday."

Bhodi gifts me one last pass of his thumb. Then he releases my hand and a cold breeze washes over me. As if the weather objects to him not touching me anymore. "What do you need to do in the church? Is this the greetings card drop?"

I find my voice. "Not quite. I'm not done with those yet. This is something else."

He's interested enough that I take him inside to show him the stacks of Christmas-wrapped shoeboxes piled all over the church. Every corner, every pew, every wall.

"They get sent overseas," I explain. "I write the little cards for the French speaking communities."

Bhodi spins around, grasping the enormity of the operation I have nothing to do with other than this. "How many is that?"

"How many cards? Or how many boxes are in the church right now?"

"Both."

"I wrote eight hundred cards, but to put it in perspective, around seven thousand boxes pass through here every year."

Bhodi whistles and crouches to look at a few. I leave him to it and find the drop-off point for the cards.

I'm gone less than five minutes.

I come back to find him eating cake, another clutched in his hand.

"Take it." He thrusts it at me. "This is my second one already."

"Hungry?"

"Always."

I can fix that. I hustle him out of the church and down the road to the Christmas fair I'd planned on avoiding since I got in a punch-up there last year. *For Rudy*. It's no wonder my dog hates all things Christmas except the chipolatas. I don't mind punching someone twice, but I don't want Bhodi to see that side of me. "You like turkey?"

It's noisy at the fair, light and laughter everywhere we turn. Bhodi leans closer to hear me. "What's that?"

I decide it's easier to show him and steer him to the food truck doling out roast dinners in Yorkshire pudding wraps.

His face lights up and I think I love him.

Avoir le coup de foudre.

Fucking hell.

I buy Bhodi dinner.

He buys me a big fat cookie for after, and we sit and eat with pints of shit lager from the other pub—not the one I had a fight outside last year.

I like watching Bhodi eat, and I'm starting to lose count of how many times I've thought that over the past few weeks. Of how often I zone out and picture his smile, even when he's right in front of me like he is right now.

"Does it still hurt?"

"What?"

Bhodi balls up the cookie box and fires it into his empty

pint glass, Christmas lights twinkling in his blue eyes. "Your hand."

I glance down and find I'm pressing my own thumb into the spot Bhodi unlocked as my new kryptonite. "It's fine. It just feels nice."

"Nice is good, right?"

"Better than good. Is that a nurse thing? Rubbing people's hands?"

Bhodi nods. "Some of the patients I see have been incapacitated a long time. Acupressure can help with the discomfort that causes."

"I didn't know that."

Neither did any medical professional I've ever come across, but I keep that to myself and focus on how close we're sitting—how close we *always* sit. We're at a picnic bench in the town square, but I could be comfortable anywhere with Bhodi. He makes my heart beat like an incoming storm, but I like the wildness I feel around him. The recklessness, when I've spent so long drowning in caution, too scared to face any more pain.

He'll never hurt me.

Course he won't. He's my *friend.*

"Something funny?"

I dust crumbs from my hands, absorbing Bhodi's nearness. The warmth seeping from his body, and the piney-cotton scent that makes me think of clean sheets beneath a fir tree. A big bed in the woods. Him and me. Me and him. "Nothing's funny, except my silly brain."

Bhodi leans back—he's facing away from the table, facing *me*—and stretches his legs out, his strong thigh so very nearly pressed to mine. "What are you thinking about?"

"How I've never thought about a friend as much as I think about you."

The smile of my dreams comes back, but it's tinged with something that makes my body *scream* with the urge to reach for him. "That word's been spinning around my head too," he admits. "I like it—I *need* it—but I still want to fuck you."

It's the first time either of us has said it out loud, and it should feel out of context. Too sudden, too soon, but it doesn't. Because I want to fuck him too...almost as much as I want to be his friend. His person. His fucking rock. And that keeps me in my seat when my baser instincts want to lean in and kiss the shit out of him.

"But we can't bang." Bhodi keeps talking when I don't. "You're my landlord. It'd be like a bad porno."

Despite the echo of Sab's thoughts on the matter, I remain convinced that nothing about banging Bhodi could ever be bad, but the scenario he's describing is still seven shades of awful. I really am his fucking landlord. I'm in a position of power. If this went south, Bhodi's the vulnerable one.

I knock his knee with mine. "I know all that. Doesn't stop me thinking about it."

"Oh yeah?" Mischief dances in Bhodi's gaze. "What are we doing? And how are we doing it?"

I press my finger to my lips. "Shh. There's kids around."

There aren't. Not really. But I'm not sure I can put words to the daydreams that blow through my brain when I'm least prepared for them. Bhodi's a dirty bastard, I can tell, but would he want me like that? On my fucking—

"You're a tease."

Bhodi rises, breaking me out of wherever the fuck *that*

thought was going. He towers over me, which doesn't help, but I'm here for it. I'm here for anything except annoying him.

Have I done that? With his face cast in shadow from a nearby streetlight, it's hard to tell, and I don't like not knowing.

I swing my legs from under the bench and stand, swallowing the distance Bhodi's put between us. He's fractionally shorter than me, but a little wider, a cast-iron fact that does nothing to help me rein this shit in. "Sorry if I'm making this weird."

"You're not." Bhodi hooks the cord of my hoodie around his finger before he seems to catch himself and let it go. "I'm just not used to...I don't know. Holding back, I suppose. I usually plough on whether it's a good idea or not, and that's what I'm trying to stop doing. And with *you*, it matters even more that I don't fuck it up."

"Why's that?"

Discord sullies his gaze again, fighting with what might be shyness, but I can't be sure. "I like you, Tam. Being around you makes me feel good, and I haven't felt that with someone in... actually, I'm not sure I've ever felt it."

I take a breath to tell him I feel the same. That I want him more than I've ever wanted anyone, but that I'm scared too. Of losing the easy companionship that comes so naturally to us. Of losing his gentle touch, and beautiful fucking smile.

But Bhodi's phone blares, shattering the moment, and I step back to let him reach for it.

It's work. I can tell by the seriousness that descends on him. I give him even more space and contemplate the crêpe stall. I can make better at home, but my sweet tooth is the vice I can indulge right now, and the longer Bhodi is away from me, the more the scent of sugar, butter, and spiced citrus gets to me.

Fuck it.

I buy one and Bhodi catches me as I'm shoving the first bite in my mouth.

"Cute."

"What is?"

"The sugar on your lips." Bhodi thumbs it off. "You should bottle that image and sell it to cheer people up."

"You need cheering up?"

"Not now."

I study him, trying to gauge what could've happened in the last three minutes to kill his mood. "Everything okay at work?"

Bhodi shrugs. "Yeah, just the day team trying to decipher my writing. It's a problem everywhere I go."

We've talked about this before, but without the subtle dejection weighing Bhodi down now. "If it's any consolation, I can read it just fine."

"You're the only one." Bhodi takes the bite of crêpe I offer him, and I see his point as sugar coats his lips too. "I don't know what it is—*I* can read just fine too, but for writing, it's like my brain and my hand aren't connected. I had to take all my nursing exams in a special room with a laptop."

"But you passed them."

He nods. "I knew my shit—I *still* know my shit. That's why it pisses me off so much when people talk to me like I'm thick as mince."

His frustration shouldn't be this attractive. But then everything about Bhodi riles me up, and maybe this is the one thing I can act on without giving oxygen to the smouldering burn between us.

I drive us home. Bhodi shakes off his bad mood and gives me a playful kiss on the cheek before he heads for the side gate.

Don't ask him in. Don't ask him in. Don't ask him in.

I resist. Just. But I call after him anyway. "Are you working tomorrow?"

"Day shift."

Which means he'll be home around four. I won't be done by then, but for what I have in mind, it won't matter. "Find me after, okay? I've got something to show you."

Ten

BHODI

Come find me after turns out to be later than planned. By two days. I finish late on the first, and on the second, every time I look in on Tam, he's gone.

We keep just missing each other, and for whatever reason, we've never got round to exchanging numbers, and digging it out of my tenancy paperwork feels kinda wrong.

"You have glitter in your hair." Tam waves me into his house, his feet bare to the rustic floorboards.

"Better than blood on my hands."

"Has it been that kind of day?"

"Actually, no." I hang my coat and toe off my Vans. "I got roped into decorating the ward on my day off, and I stole you some Frosty Fancies to make up for airing you the other day."

Tam takes the box and tears into it, stuffing a sparkly-white cake straight into his mouth. "How did you know?"

"Know what?"

"That I ate all my Bakewells at lunchtime." Tam wipes his

mouth with the back of his tattooed hand. "And you don't need to make up for shit. When you didn't show, I figured you'd got stuck at work, and then you didn't come back till the middle of the night, so I didn't want to bug you."

"You couldn't bug me if you tried."

"Sounds like a challenge." Tam offers me the box.

I wave it away only because I've already eaten a hundred cakes today, snaffling up donations left by local charities most of the patients on the ward are too unwell to eat.

At least, that's what I told myself, and three hours into lugging crap from storage to the ward, I'd stopped caring. "What did you want to show me?"

Tam ditches the cakes and points to the stairs.

I cock a brow.

Tam simmers his russet gaze at me. His *amused* gaze. "It's way less exciting than whatever you're thinking."

"You have no idea what I'm thinking."

Bet he does. And the smirk Tam tosses over his shoulder as he leads me to the stairs says the same. But I follow him anyway, up the wooden staircase, taking in the art work and photographs that punctuate the walls, breathing deeper as that cinnamon scent gets stronger.

His bedroom is up here. And the door is closed. But the studio door is wide open and I'm as drawn to it now as I was the first time I came up here. "Wow." I glance around. "There's so much going on in here."

Tam gives a weary chuckle. "Tell me about it. I don't know where anything is anymore."

"Was it better in the annex? It must be weird not leaving the house to go to work anymore."

"I don't miss tramping across the garden sixty times a day."

"Sixty?"

"Rudy turns into a massive wanker when he can't throw himself at the front door every time someone walks past the house. Won't shut the fuck up until I let him check they're gone. When I'm up here, he can sort himself out."

"Fair enough. What did you want to show me?"

Tam moves a stack of cards to one side and opens a drawer. From inside, he grabs a slim black box and what looks like a notebook. "Come here."

It's instinct to obey without question, and I don't mind. Especially as where he wants me to be is right next to him. "Is that a schoolbook?"

"Nearly." Tam flips the pages, revealing reams and reams of carol lyrics and festive stories printed in faint cursive. "You see these guidelines?"

I wince. "They look like the torture books from primary school."

"Not far off, but it's not torture, I promise. Come here."

Again.

And of course, I obey as he steers me to a second desk that's less cluttered than the one that seems to be his main workstation.

"Hold this pen. See how it feels."

He's serious. I purse my lips as he presses a red and gold stylus-type thing into my writing hand and manoeuvres my fingers into a position a world away from how I usually hold a pen. "What kind of pen is this?"

Tam grins. "Don't ask me questions like that. I might answer, and you're a busy man."

"You like pens?"

"My job would be pretty shit if I didn't." Tam fills the space beside me and resets the workbook on the table at the very first page. Letters, not words. Loads of them. Line after line. Enough to make my head swim. "Can you write something here for me?"

"Like what?"

"Whatever you want. Or something you have trouble writing at work."

"That would be everything. Even my own name."

"So write that."

He's joking, he has to be. But I can't think of anything else, so I scratch out the drug order I got in trouble for a few days ago, fighting with the odd angle of the gold nib. All with Tam watching over my shoulder, silent and still, his warmth seeping into me like a hug.

I love it.

I hate it.

I love it some more as I sign off with my name and he leans closer still. "That do you?"

"Write something else. A longer sentence."

"Are you testing my grammar?"

"Fuck, no."

"Thank the Lord." I frown at the page and scrawl what's on my mind.

Three words.

You smell nice.

Tam laughs. "Thanks."

"It's true. I thought it way back when I met you in the car park."

"That's funny. I thought you looked like a fucking angel, until I saw the hospital ID. Then I thought the devil had come back for me."

Tam speaks absently as he scrutinises the mess I've made on the pristine inside cover of the book. I hold my breath in case he says more.

He doesn't. At least, not about that. He points to the first row of letters on the page. "Try tracing these."

"Why?"

"I'm trying to see which part of configuring the words glitches for you."

"My whole brain glitches."

"No, it doesn't. You do these combinations just fine. See here?" He points to the word *you*. "That's pretty fucking perfect."

"You have strange ideas of perfection."

Tam says nothing. Just watches my cack-handed attempt to string letters together with a frown that should maybe feel critical, but doesn't.

He reaches around me, his chest to my back, and grips my wrist, adjusting the angle of the nib, guiding me across the page. It takes a few lines. More than a few. Then something clicks and the pen seems steer itself, gliding over the paper like butter.

I find myself spellbound. And gobsmacked letters that neat came from my hand, even with Tam's soft grip on my wrist. "Wow. That's almost legible."

Tam makes a sound low in his throat.

That's it. No admonishment. No praise. Just a low rumble of *shut the fuck up and write.*

So I do. I turn the pages and keep going, even after he lets go of my wrist and steps back. I keep writing until I get to a poem about Santa needing a new reindeer.

It makes me think of Rudy. I scan the room for him and find him on Tam's shoulder, his sharp gaze trained on the garden while Tam works, and it's quite the view. *My* idea of perfect. So I let myself stare and stare and stare, until I find myself drawn in by the casual dichotomy of Tam's rough, tattooed hand and the elegant art that flows from it.

Intricate.

Delicate.

It shouldn't fit, but it does.

I ease away from my desk and pad up behind him, hypnotised by the dance of his pen across the parchment, and the inky beauty left in its wake. The *swift* dance. He pens a verse onto a greetings card in the time it takes me to form a single word. Then he's onto the next, over and over, a production line that doesn't come up for air. "You should've been a surgeon."

Tam pauses. "Blood makes me puke."

"Is that why the hospital freaks you out?"

Tam takes a breath and carries on writing—a subtle hint for me to shut the hell up, or he's too busy to stop while I poke at him. Either way, I don't expect him to answer, and I'm halfway back to the other desk when he does. "I don't like that hospital because I died there a couple of times after a bike crash."

I freeze, horror squeezing my heart, the flash of that scar on his back invading my mind. "When?"

"Six years ago."

"What happened?"

"Can you come here again?"

I return to the space behind him. "Where do you need me?"

Tam's hot smirk returns, fainter than usual, but pronounced enough that I know he's still in there. "Right there would be good, but for this, I need to see you."

There's no room to consider the implications of *right there*. I move to Tam's side, eating up the inches between us until we're touching, until he can feel me. Then he takes another breath, his pen still weaving across the page, and the words seem to flow with every dip and swirl of the nib.

"I was riding home from a messy break-up. It was around this time of year, actually, and the weather was all over the place. Snow one day, sunshine and showers the next."

"Black ice?"

Tam hums. "Yeah. And I knew it, but I was distracted—I was *angry*, and I was driving like a prick." He stops to scrutinise the sentence he's just written. Goes back and extends the tail on the letter *Y.* "I mean, everyone was, but if I'd had my head screwed on right, I'd have seen the taxi burning up the slip road behind me."

I lean closer, instinct, not a conscious decision, and it narrows the paper-thin space between us to nothing. My shoulder eases against his, and it's a perfect press of flesh and bone. Solid. Warm. Like the soft smile he sends my way, even through the hurt simmering in his gaze.

Tam starts writing again. "The taxi took me out. Sent me flying into the path of another car already on the motorway. Fucked my back and mashed my liver."

"Your liver?"

He sets his pen down mid-word and tugs his shirt up. I'm expecting the road burn scars. The faded white line of a liver resection catches me off guard.

I reach for it without stopping to make sense of what I'm doing. Trace it with my fingertip as Tam shivers at my touch. "That's some major surgery." One that lets me know he really did almost die. How lucky I am to have ever met him. "Any after-effects?"

"Not often. About twice a year I get so tired I pretty much

fall into a coma for a couple of days, but I don't know for sure that it's related."

"Probably is." I trace the scar again. Another shiver skitters through Tam's torso. "It's sensitive?"

"Not that I knew of before you fucking touched me."

I let my hand drop.

Tam grips my wrist and brings it back. "I like it."

I like it too, and it's a struggle to keep my head in the game. If we'd been talking about anything else...

But the gravity of that white line and what it means isn't lost on me, and I let myself glance over the other marks on his body. There's a tattoo on his back too marred by surface scars to be recognisable. My fingers skim it, and this time, Tam groans.

"And you say I'm a fucking tease."

"Not on purpose." I grit my teeth and tug his shirt down, though I don't back up. "You had a spinal injury too?"

"Fracture at the bottom somewhere. It's fine now unless I sit down too long. That's why I work at standing desks."

"I thought you were just trendy."

"Really?" Tam's brows knit together in a dry frown. "I wouldn't know trendy if it bit me in the arse."

"Don't put biting you in my head."

I'm joking. Mostly. Or, not at all as Tam stares me down. Knowing how bad he was hurt isn't easy, but if there's one thing that can pull me out of picturing him half-dead on a hospital bed, it's imagining how the hot skin of his throat would feel beneath my lips. How he'd taste. How—

Stop.

I try, I do, but Tam doesn't play ball. He just keeps staring, and we're drawn together with the same voracity as all bad ideas. The same compulsive thrill. Our lips brush. Once. Twice.

A third time that cranks up the heat to a dangerous swelter as his hands come to my face and mine return to his perfectly imperfect torso.

I'm knee-deep in tugging him against me before I get a hold of myself. "Shit. Sorry."

Tam rumbles that low sound again. Then lets me go. "I'm not fucking sorry."

"No?"

"Why would I be sorry?"

"Because—" Actually, I have no idea. About anything, save the fact that it's probably time I left.

"Come and have a cup of tea with me."

Say no. Go home.

Doesn't happen. We wind up on Tam's couch. He breaks out the Mr Kipling I brought him earlier and goads me into eating them too.

"I'm not sorry I kissed you upstairs." He leans back on the couch, shifting a little in a way I now recognise as someone with a grumpy lumbar spine. "But I won't ever do it again if it makes you uncomfortable."

"The only uncomfortable thing is my jeans."

His gaze darts to my groin.

I flick his knee. "Made you look."

He laughs and it breaks any lingering tension. Not that there was much, and I realise I'm not sorry either.

I correct the record.

Tam laughs some more and I feel myself relax in ways I didn't the whole time I was with Skylar.

You were never with Skylar. And you'll never be with Tam either.

Because he doesn't do relationships, and I've sworn off

114

them for good, even if the mere thought of it turns the sugar coursing through my veins to scratchy dust particles. So I don't think about it. I think about something else—about what people who don't commit to relationships do instead.

I think about *sex*, and it's a mistake. A hard one, pushing against the zip of my jeans.

Jesus Christ.

Tam nudges me. "You okay?"

"Yep."

"Really? You look stressed."

"I have resting stress face."

"T'as des beaux yeux."

"What?"

"No, you don't."

I remember enough of school French to know he absolutely did not say that. But I'm distracted by the arch of his neck as he stretches it, and that overwhelming need to kiss him there.

Resisting takes a marathon effort and a hassled sigh escapes me.

Tam cocks his head. "What are you thinking?"

"Thinking?"

"You have a hundred thoughts raging in your head. I can see them."

"Then you should already know what I'm thinking."

"Be better if you told me."

"Why?"

Tam licks sugary icing from his thumb. "Lots of reasons. You want them all?"

"Give me one."

"It's a selfish fucking reason."

"Selfish of me?"

115

"Fuck. No. Definitely me." He's suddenly closer again. "But you're a tough crowd for bullshit so I'm going to tell you anyway."

I wait.

He cracks his knuckles and shrugs. "I was thinking about you fucking me and feeling guilty about it. So I was wondering if that missile in your jeans means you've been thinking about it too."

I choke on my tea. "Me fucking you?"

"What makes you say it like that?"

"Er…" But that's it. I have nothing else coherent. Just a thousand *more* wild thoughts fighting for dominance in my already crowded brain, and none of them do the cramped space in my jeans any favours. "I was thinking about *you* fucking me," I eventually admit. "I haven't topped in a long time."

"Me either."

It shouldn't surprise me. I know better than to judge a man's sexual preference by how he looks. But I do it anyway and my head spins off my shoulders. "Thanks for the new imagery."

Tam laughs. "Well, I guess it's a good thing we're never going to fuck, eh? We won't have to fight over it."

"You're wrong," I say slowly.

As slowly as Tam's dark brow edges up. "Wrong about what?"

"The bit about fighting over it." I press my fist to his thigh and rise, knowing I really do need to leave before I combust. "Because if *we* were fucking? Trust me, I'd make an exception."

Eleven

TAM

"If we were fucking? Trust me, I'd make an exception."

The words play on repeat in my head for hours after Bhodi leaves.

Days, in fact.

A week and a half.

Because it's that long before I get to see him again in any real capacity. Bhodi's shift pattern works against us. Then I wake up one morning to find Sab asleep on my sofa, his baby girl in a travel cot behind him, and everything's fucked.

For him, at least.

I kick his foot for the tenth time in the past hour. "What the fuck are you doing with your life?"

Sab grunts, still ankle-deep in whatever drove him to walk out on his missus and drive all the way here.

He's not hurt.

Physically.

But for the first time in years, I have no idea where his head is at. "Did you relapse?"

"What?"

"*Relapse*," I repeat, balancing Esme on my hip. She's half asleep and way less annoying than her dad. "As in—"

"I know what you meant."

Sab shoves to his feet and stomps to the kitchen.

He comes back with the ragout I'd had grand plans to share with Bhodi tonight if he made it home from the hospital before I passed out. Or for breakfast if it's the only time I catch him. Now it's Sab's brunch and I'm as irritated about that as I am about his sudden need to be fucking coy.

"Stop eating my food and tell me what the fuck's going on."

"Where's your Christmas tree?"

"I haven't done it yet."

"Why not?"

"Because—" Because I've been waiting for Bhodi to come and choose one with me. *Because* I know it's one of his favourite parts of Christmas, and he's probably going to miss everything else. "Don't change the subject."

Sab sets his bowl down and sends me a flat look. "Why would I confide in you when the first thing you think is that I've been on the fucking sniff?"

"It's the only thing you've ever lied to me about."

"You think I'm lying?"

"No, I think you're being a fucking weirdo and that usually means you've fucked something up." I want to shout. But with Esme in my arms, all I manage is a barbed whisper. And maybe, that's why he brought her. To use as a human shield. "Does Charmaine know you're here?"

"Charmaine doesn't care where I go."

118

"She cares about Esme."

Sab snorts. "Does she?"

"Far as I know. You want to tell me something different?"

Sab glares at the floorboards.

I want to punch him, so I retreat upstairs with Esme and put her down for a nap in the cot that's already migrated to my bedroom. For her sake, not his. Though, I'd give my brother my bed in a heartbeat. My whole house and everything in it.

I'd give him my patience if I had any.

Newsflash: I don't.

I get in his face the second I'm back downstairs. "Fucking tell me."

"She's been knocking off that dickhead from the gym."

I search my brain for anyone and everyone Sab's complained about. It's a short list. My brother's a nice bloke—nicer than *me* —and one name sticks out. "Dwaine? With the disco pump arms?"

"That's the prick. She's been banging him for two years."

Two years. I do the maths and my stomach drops. "That's longer than you've been together."

"Yup."

"But..." I glance at the ceiling.

Sab grimaces. "Yup. But it's okay. I checked. She's mine."

"How did you check?"

"DNA test when Char was "at her mum's" for the night. I felt fucking unhinged when I was doing it, but it was okay in the end."

My heart retreats from the wild gallop it leaned into while I contemplated losing Esme. *Sab* losing Esme. "That's—"

"It doesn't matter," Sab growls. "She's my kid, and I wouldn't have cared if the test had said any different."

119

I don't doubt him. Not for one second. But I'm not naïve enough to believe it would've been that easy. Nothing ever is. "What are you going to do?"

Sab lapses into muttering in French. I give him the mental space to do it, all the while knowing I won't leave his side, and *of course*, it's the moment I hear Bhodi's car pull up outside.

Rudy hears him too. He likes Bhodi and he goes to the door to whine and wait on the mat, assuming Bhodi will at least knock to say hello.

But I know he won't. Sab's van will put him off, and a wrench twists my stomach.

I miss him, I realise. At some point over the past month or so, he's become a non-negotiable in my life. *And we've barely kissed.* Because we're *friends*.

"That the hot lodger?"

I retune to find Sab has hauled his spurned self off the couch and moved to the window, and it annoys me that he can see Bhodi and I can't. "Mind your own business."

Sab swivels to face me. "You're banging him, aren't you?"

"No."

"No?"

"*No.*" I rise and drag Sab from the window. "How did you leave things with Charmaine?"

"I punched her fancy man. She called me a closet bender."

"Why would she say that?"

Sab sighs. "Because I told her once upon a time that I'd happily fuck a bloke if I ever met one that turned my head. I was drunk, and I forgot about it. She used it as an excuse to go running back to Captain Roid. Then she got knocked up and knew it was mine, so...I guess she only stayed with me because of Esme."

"That's the only reason you stayed with *her*."

"I know, but at least I tried to make it work. Treated her like a fucking queen, all while she's making digs about you, about me, and everything about us. But I'd never have cheated on her, Tam. I'd have offed myself before I did that to the mother of my kid."

He's come close before, to killing himself. It's been years, but I can't forget it. I pull him into a hug and squeeze him tight, letting my irritation bleed out of me. "It's going to be okay. You can stay with me as long as you need."

Sab lets me hold him. Then he backs off. "She's not going to let me hole up here with Esme. I have to go back."

"You need money? I can help you put a deposit down on a place."

"With what? You're as skint as I am."

"You can have the annex money."

"No."

I'm the stubborn one, but I know Sab, and for now, there's no changing his mind. I leave him to his foraged brunch and head upstairs to work.

It's mid-afternoon when I blink out of an ink daze to see Bhodi leaving the annex.

He's in running gear, which I like. But the pavements are icy as hell, a definite *fuck no*.

I push back from my desk and jog downstairs. Sab is on the rug in front of the log burner, playing with Esme. He shoots me a knowing look. I ignore him and dash outside barefoot. "Hey."

Bhodi spins around, startled, and it makes his eyes impossibly brighter. Like gemstones in the fucking snow. "Hey."

"Going running?"

"No, I just really like leggings."

"You're not wearing leggings."

"I am underneath. It's cold."

"It's *icy*. You got crampons for those pretty feet?"

He grins. "You think my feet are pretty?"

"If they're anything like the rest of you."

Bhodi laughs into a broad grin. "Charmer. Where've you been all my life?"

Waiting for you. "Be careful, okay? It's getting dark."

His smile fades a little. "I will, I promise. Everything all right?"

I can't lie to him. "Sab's having life drama. Him and the baby are holed up in my place."

"Baby?"

"My niece. Esme. I didn't tell you about her?"

"You might've done." Bhodi blows on his hands. "I get a bit empty-headed around you."

"Oh yeah? Why's that?"

"Because *you're* pretty, Dubois."

I feel like a new man. All day I've vacillated between missing him and worrying about Sab. Now I'm ten seconds deep with him and my smile hurts my face. "Are you home tonight?"

Bhodi nods. "Unless I get called in. Everyone's got norovirus, so it might happen if the ward loses too many of the night shift. Why?"

I don't actually know. Sab isn't going anywhere, but the thought of not seeing Bhodi for however long my brother needs me is enough to kill my smile.

Bhodi steps closer. "Sure you're okay?"

"Yeah."

He eyes me for a long moment, then brushes a cautious kiss

to my cheek. "Hey, I'm in all night. Come find me if you need something. And wear shoes when you do."

When. Not if. And Bhodi's gone before my imagination can run wild with that one, leaving me to trudge back inside to face Sab. He hasn't moved, but he doesn't have to bear witness to every second of my life to read me. "He does something to you."

I'm tired of denying it. I stretch out on the rug and tweak Esme's dark, Dubois curls. "I know."

"Something good?"

"Maybe."

Sab snorts. "It's definitely something good. I've never seen you chase after someone like that. And you've been waiting to catch sight of him all day."

"I don't have his number."

"He kissed you."

"You kiss me all the time."

"I'm your brother." Sab plants a smacker on my cheek. "And we're French. But if you looked at me the way you were looking at him, I'd call the police."

"Fuck off."

Sab hums, thinking, which is always dangerous. "How did you leave it?"

"Leave what?"

"Whatever fuckwit conversation you treated him to outside."

The baby stops me poking him. I steal her and sit her on my chest, ignoring the ache in my back that's been grumbling since I told Bhodi about the accident. As if it wants to remind me of something I haven't figured out yet. "I asked if he was in later."

"And?"

"*And*, he said he was."

"Please tell me you're going to go over there and kiss him back."

"What makes you think he wasn't kissing *me* back?"

Sab laughs, though it's dimmed by the stress lining his face. "Fucking knew it."

"You don't know anything."

"I know *you*. And as your favourite sibling, it's my responsibly to make sure you don't Tam your way out of something that makes you giddy enough to run out the door half-dressed."

"I'm dressed."

"Your jeans are undone."

"No, they're not."

"Whatever. My point stands. Don't waste this, mon frère. You deserve better than that. Maybe you both do."

It's on the tip of my tongue to quip that Bhodi deserves better than *me*. And that Sab's my only fucking sibling, so he's my favourite by default. But my mind skips past all that too fast for me to verbalise, too eager to get to the good shit—the possibility that I get to see Bhodi again today. The certainty, actually. There's no doubt in my mind I'll be knocking on his door before this day is over.

The real question is how long I can hold out.

Twelve

BHODI

I've made a vow not to waste another second of my life waiting on a call that never comes. Metaphorically, obviously. Tam still doesn't have my number. And he hasn't asked for it. So I don't let myself wait up for him. Or glance away from the TV any time I sense movement outside.

I do what I always do when I'm home for the night—home *alone*. I eat noodles, take a shower, and crawl into bed to doze in front of the telly. *Don't think about Tam.* And I don't for the most part. I shut my mind off with the iron will I need to learn from the past, and I'm pretty much asleep when a light tap on the annex door rouses me somewhere between Eastenders ending and some hospital documentary taking over.

I'd rather stick pins in my eyes than watch a show about work in my downtime.

I fumble the remote as I drift, bare-chested, to the door, and switch the channel to who knows what.

Then I open the door and forget all about it. About everything except the man hiding behind his hood.

Tam.

Which means he's hiding from the snow, not me. Skylar used his hood to shut the whole world out. Tam's different. He tips it back and smiles like I'm the best thing he's ever seen, and something inside me settles.

"Come in." I step aside, yawning. "It's freezing out there."

Tam hesitates. "Did I wake you up?"

"No."

"There are pillow lines on your face."

"I was resting my eyes, and I'm off tomorrow. Come *in*."

Tam steps over the threshold and toes off his boots. He unzips his hoodie too and shrugs it off, revealing the old grey T-shirt he wears a lot when he's working at home.

It bears the name of the same motorcycle club that populates Devon and Cornwall, where I used to work. "You were a Rebel King?"

Tam blinks and glances at the faded insignia on his chest. "A long time ago. Until I ate dirt and never rode again."

"They kicked you out?"

"Fuck, no." Tam ventures further inside, taking in my rumpled, unmade bed, and the lack of anywhere else to sit. "They gave me money for the deposit on the house and patched me out when I was ready. I could've stayed if I wanted to. It's a brotherhood—they take care of their own."

It fits with what little I know about the Rebel Kings MC. But to tell Tam that breaks patient confidentiality, so I move to the kitchen and grab a couple of beers.

Tam hovers by my bed.

I pass him a bottle and flop down, waiting, letting him figure it out himself.

A few loaded beats pass before he claims the other side and reclines against the pillows.

He's my landlord and he's in bed with me. But it doesn't feel weird. I lounge beside him and drink my beer while he frowns at the TV.

"You're watching Porridge?"

Apparently so. "I have a prison kink."

Tam chuckles. "You'd like some of my old mates then."

"From the club?"

"Yeah. I was pretty tame by their standards, but I rode with some characters."

"I can't picture you as a gangster."

Tam snorts. "Good."

"Does that mean you weren't one?"

"It means I wasn't much of one."

He's smiling again, so I can't tell if he's joking. And I decide it doesn't matter. I like this version of Tam. Who he was ten years ago is only as important as he wants it to be.

"How's Sab?"

I turn my head as I ask the question. He mirrors the action and it brings us face to face, intimately close on the compact sofa bed. "I think he's gay."

It's the last thing I expect him to say. And I've learned with Tam, to give him a minute to define what he means.

"Sab's as into men as I am," Tam elaborates. "But he's never explored it. Every time I think he's going to, he ends up in a relationship that blows up in his face."

"Like this one?"

Tam purses his lips and takes an inhale through his nose. "I don't like saying bad things about Esme's mum."

"It's not a crime to not like someone."

"You can tell I don't like her?"

I want to reach for Tam so bad my fingers twitch. So I do it, smoothing the divot between his brows without comment.

He smiles a little, and I'm so here for that, even though it's fleeting before his expression sobers again. "Charmaine's not good for Sab. I always thought she got pregnant on purpose, so she had something to hold over him. Or a backup plan if whatever she was really gunning for didn't work out."

"What do you think now?"

"I think she's a toxic bitch—a toxic *person*—who cheated on my brother. And I feel like a cunt for being relieved she did because I want him away from her."

"You'd be more of a cunt if you didn't want him away from something that's bad for him."

Tam nods, slowly. "That's how I knew from the start she didn't care about him. Sab had a coke habit way back when. It's how he ended up at the church. He's been clean years, but it's still not okay to rack up lines on the coffee table around him, you know?"

"She did that?"

"A few months back. Her and her mates piled into the house for a mad one. Didn't give a fuck that he was right here with the baby."

"That's awful."

"Yup." Tam sighs and pushes his hair back with his good hand. "Like, I couldn't do that to a stranger. To *you*, the split second we met, and Sab...he's got his faults, but he's the best brother I could ever have. It makes no fucking sense to me that she can't love him how he deserves."

"Would he want that from her if she did?"

"I don't know. Sab's not like me. He needs more than a hookup. But he always picks shockers to invest in."

"What about you? What's your track record like?"

"Recently?" Tam gives me a shameless once-over. "Impeccable. But I've fucked up too, plenty of times. The dude I was riding away from the night of the accident slept with my boss."

"Ouch."

Tam shrugs it off. "I got over it pretty quick. I had other things on my mind. What about you? I know this other bloke messed with your head, but what was your life like before that?"

"Probably a lot like Sab's, minus the blow habit and babies." The wind whistles outside, gusting snow against the windowpanes, reminding me that I still haven't figured out the log burner. "Are you cold?"

"I'm in bed with you."

"*On* the bed." Though his version of reality has So. Much. Appeal. "I can light the fire—maybe. I've never tried."

"At all, or just here?"

"At all."

Tam takes my hand and rises so fast I don't realise it's happening until I'm standing on two socked feet. He guides me to the unused log burner and lets go to open it. "Logs are out the back."

By the door I haven't got round to opening. I pad over and retrieve a couple. They're cold and tough to my palms. Damp, even. But Tam says nothing as I pile them beside him, too busy scrunching paper and stacking little sticks like Jenga.

He lights the fire and loads the logs. Instant heat hits my face, but I know that, like Tam, the real warmth lies deeper, and I'm prepared to wait. The question is where. Having him stretched out on my bed is heaven, but I'd be lying if I don't admit I've wasted *hours* to daydreaming about rolling around on the floor with him too.

I reclaim his hand. "Sit? Unless it hurts your back..."

In answer, Tam folds his tall frame onto the rug.

We've left our beers by the bed.

I assume that's what he gets up for a split-second later. Then shadows cloak the annex and I realise he's...shut the blinds. "Oh damn. I didn't know they were there."

"And here's me thinking you were just an exhibitionist."

Tam hands me my beer. His gaze is hot, and I wonder what he's seen. Then decide I don't care. If it bothered him, he'd have told me about the blinds a month ago. Which begs the question...

Why's he closing them now?

Or, more likely, why am *I* thinking it's for any reason other than it's dark?

Tam sits down again. He stares at me, then swipes his thumb between my brows the way I did him a few minutes ago. "What are you thinking so hard about?"

"Me? Nothing."

He rumbles the low sound that makes my blood pump a little hotter.

Leans closer.

Then he sits back with a quiet sigh. "I've missed you."

I miss him now he's half a foot further away. And this week?

Wow. After the evening we spent together in his spare bedroom and on his couch, he's been on my mind constantly.

Even at work, where I've been trying to put into practice the writing skills from his books. Especially at work. I've had some really sick patients to look after this week, and it's made me think of Tam, and how close I came to losing him before I ever met him. "I missed you too."

"My cooking or my amazing sense of humour?"

"All of it." I lie back on the rug, instinct telling me he'll do the same.

He does, and he reaches for me again, except this time, it's not to chase away whatever frown is creasing my face, it's to cup my cheek and brush his thumb over my cheekbone.

This is dangerous.

Tam doesn't want how he's making me feel. He likes me. We're friends. And he wants to fuck—I *know* that. But that's it. These butterflies in my stomach? They have to fly the hell away. Or I need to find the will to stop him touching me like this, and I already know I don't have it.

"You asked about my track record." My voice is a whisper. "It's messy, I can't lie. But maybe it's time I got better at picking who to fuck."

Thirteen

TAM

"Maybe it's time I got better at picking who to fuck."

Bhodi's killing me with these one-liners. Except this time, he doesn't leave. He can't, because we're at his place, on his rug, in front of his fire, and it's down to me to end this before it begins. To smother the growing flame between us before it burns out of control.

But I'm as weak as I am stubborn and I keep my hand on his face, hooked by the spark in his bright eyes.

The heat.

I want him.

For more than a peck on the cheek and some gentle flirtation.

I want to be his fucking exception.

Kissing him is so easy, I don't truly grasp how it happens. Just that the moment to stare at each other passes, and then my mouth is on his, my tongue slipping between his lips, and I stop thinking about the consequences of messing around with my tenant.

I pull him on top of me.

Surprise stutters his kiss, but he goes with it, bracing an arm on the rug as his broader frame weighs me down. "This doesn't hurt you?"

I bite his lips. "No."

Bhodi smiles, but it's consumed by the rising inferno between us.

He's wearing fuck-all. Just sweats and socks. No underwear, I can tell, and it dizzies me knowing only a scrap of cotton lies between me and the solid heat he's packing. The hardness already digging into my leg.

I reach for it.

He catches my hands, pinning them above my head, careful with my cast, but firm enough with his touch that I know I'm in trouble when this gets going. "Did you mean what you said the other night?"

"Which part?"

"The part about switching."

His gaze darkens. "Depends."

"On?"

"If *you* meant what you said."

"I meant it." He speaks without hesitation. My own cock reacts and I know he feels it. Can tell by the snake of his tongue wetting his lips. "I just never pictured it before."

It makes me wonder what he pictured instead, but I read between the lines of what he's asking me and give him the truth.

"I've always been vers, but after the accident, when I spent so long not in control of my own body, I learned to find a thrill in giving it up. Like...not violent shit, fuck no. More a subtle dominance? If that's a thing—I don't know how else to describe it."

Bhodi takes a slow breath, contemplation swirling in his gaze as he squeezes my hands, tightening his grip on them. "I think I know what you mean."

"Yeah?"

"Yeah."

Bhodi kisses me, and it's different this time. The sweetness has gone, and in its place is a rough fire that spins me out as much as the descending weight of his body does.

He was holding back, I realise, when I rolled him on top of me. But he's not holding back now, and I funnel my hand into his hair, arching my neck as he goes for my throat.

With his mouth.

With his teeth.

Fuck.

Arousal bolts through me. I've craved this since I met him, but I'm not fucking ready for it. I'm not *ready* for the wild sensation his attention drives through me. For the perfect fit of his body moving against mine, or the sheer compulsion that throws my leg over his hip, hooking him closer.

I'm not ready for the smooth warmth of his skin.

Bhodi tugs my shirt over my head. He has to release my hands to do it, but I leave them where they are. If I touch him right now, I'll explode, and I want to see how far he takes this.

Where he starts.

Where he stops.

Don't fucking stop.

Bhodi looms over me. In the shadows of the room, the firelight dancing in his eyes, he's more gorgeous than ever, and my chest gives way to a heavy breath, anticipation searing my lungs.

"I like this one." He ghosts a finger over the sparrows on my chest. "It must've hurt."

"All the good things do."

"So do the bad ones." Bhodi leans down, his mouth inches from mine. "But bad things can be good too, right?"

"I think so."

"Let's see."

Fuck. Me.

I'm adding Bhodi's filthy mouth to the list of things I'm not ready for. Then his lips and teeth go to work on my torso too, and I'm so gone. It's like I've never been touched before. Like I've been starved for it my whole life and he's my fucking saviour.

A ragged groan escapes me.

Bhodi exhales a rough breath and hauls me up, pressing his forehead to mine. "How far do you want to take this?"

I give voice to the fantasy. "You decide."

He whistles through his teeth. "That's dangerous."

"Why?"

"Because I want to suck you dry."

That dizziness comes back. "I'm not gonna stop you."

"Sure about that?" Bhodi unbuttons my jeans, deft fingers working as he stares me down. "I might be shit at blowjobs."

"I might be shit at returning the favour."

"Who says I'm gonna let you?"

"You'll let me."

Bhodi dips his hand below my waistband. "You're probably right. But I'm not thinking about that right now."

"What are you thinking about?"

"Getting you naked...if that's okay?"

It's more than okay. My body is a map of scars and bad decisions, but I'm not shy. How Bhodi makes me feel is part of me, and I'm not afraid to show him.

I kiss him, flexing up into his hands.

Bhodi takes the hint and tugs my jeans and underwear down, tossing them with my socks, leaving me bare to him while the single item of clothing he's wearing is one too many.

He wears faded sweats like a dream, but they have to fucking go.

I push at his waistband. "Take them off?"

Bhodi smirks. "*You* take them off."

My mouth dries. I go for the sweats again and ease them away until I reach the hard dick standing in the way. It's the struggle of my life to not fixate on it, but somehow, I manage to manoeuvre over it until my arms aren't long enough to finish the job.

Bhodi takes over. His clothes join mine scattered on the floor around us and he comes back to me so gloriously naked I feel like my every fucking Christmas has come at once.

I mean, I knew he'd be beautiful, but *damn*. The sight of him is eons away from my wildest dreams. Those swathes of unmarked skin and muscled thighs that could easily pin me in place whether I let him or not. For a minute, anyway, and it makes me wonder if he'd enjoy me throwing him off. Or if he'd fuck me from the bottom, killing me with the same gentle smirk he's killing me with now as he lays me down again and straddles my legs, gazing at me with the same hunger in his eyes I know I have in mine.

Too fast. Too soon. But goddamn, I feel like I've been waiting on this moment my whole fucking life. This is deeper than an ill-advised hookup. Even if we never touch each other again, my heart already knows that no one will ever live up to him.

"You're thinking a lot." Bhodi leans down. "Everything okay?"

I'm so far beyond okay I don't have the words. But despite his dirty mouth, Bhodi's a sweet soul, and he deserves more than the vagueness I give everyone else. "You're so fucking hot it scares me."

Bhodi shifts, easing off me to find his place between my legs. "I'm not here to scare you."

"What are you here to do?"

"*This.*"

He claims my lips and slides his hand south, wrapping his fingers around my dick. And he's gentle at first, which really does fucking scare me. I'm in too deep with Bhodi already. If he's too nice, I'll fall in love with him for sure, and...

Bhodi presses down on me again, his forearm to my throat, gripping *tighter.* "Whatever it is, let it go."

I don't know what *it* is.

I don't know anything except that I need to be present in this moment in case I never get to live it again.

Closing my eyes, I take a breath and focus on the pulsating pleasure Bhodi's drawing from me with his skilled hand. It flows through me like water from a hot tap, warming with every pass of his palm. Every twist of his wrist. Every minute increase of pressure from his arm on my windpipe.

I can't breathe, but I don't want to. I want that light-headed oblivion. That hazy vision and heady rush. More than that, though, I want it from *him.* "Bhodi."

His name gravels from my lungs like a holy prayer.

Bhodi bites my lips, his dick digging into my thigh as he

amps it up—all of it, smirking as I let my body do whatever the fuck it wants. *Smouldering* as my leg curls around his hip. "You're so hot you scare *me*."

My good hand balls into a fist. On the other, my fingers strain against the cast, a reflex I can't fight, and I'm already close to losing it.

Because I haven't got laid in months?

No.

Bhodi has a wicked touch, and he's making me shake with a simple hand-job, but there's nothing so simple about the nuanced heat sluicing through me.

I need to get a grip.

To give something back.

Bhodi must read it in my eyes. He shakes his head. "Let me."

Let him what? Kill me?

Okay.

"Then fucking kiss me."

He does and somewhere in the wider universe, a switch is flipped. Urgency heightens. Pace. *Pressure.* I prepare myself to bust like this, but Bhodi has other ideas. He brings me to the brink, then rips his hand away, and I realise he's breathing as rough as I am. That his dick is as swollen and hard as mine.

"I want you in my mouth." I speak without thought.

Bhodi licks his lips. "Soon."

"Soon?"

"*Soon.*" He braces an arm by my head, slotting our bodies together as if we're fucking, his fingers gripping my hip, his dick sliding along mine, creating a dark friction that cranks my blood to a heart-pumping inferno. Bhodi's got rhythm, and when he fucks me, he's gonna rail me like a boss.

When? My subconscious mocks me.

I block it out and arch against Bhodi as he drives us together a little harder, and fresh sweat beads my skin, adding to the instinctive grind we roll into.

It feels like we're trapped in that cycle for hours. I nearly come so many times I lose count, but Bhodi becomes an instant expert in reading me, easing back at the last second over and over until I'm insane with the need to explode.

My chest heaves with the effort of holding myself together, and I still haven't touched his dick. Not with my hands, anyway. "I need—"

Bhodi seals my lips with his palm. "You *need* to fuck my mouth."

Putain. I lose more oxygen from my lungs. Bhodi stares me down for a blazing second. Then he's gone, descending my body, swallowing my dick before I can take a breath, enveloping me in his tight, hot throat.

"*Fuck.*" I jackknife from the rug, spearing my cock deeper.

Bhodi makes a gagging sound. I try to pull back, but he holds me in place, grabbing my hand and planting it on his head, and his words reverberate. *You need to fuck my mouth.*

He's right. For me or for him, it doesn't fucking matter. I do need this. And maybe, so does he.

I shift my hand to his jaw and cradle it, widening my legs. It puts pressure on my lower back, but I don't give a fuck. I barely notice, I'm so transfixed by his bright blue gaze blazing up at me as I give in to the primal instinct to drive my dick between his sweet lips over and over, the blood in my veins crackling with the energy of a lit firework.

My eyes roll and I struggle to stay anchored to the world, it's that fucking good. It's that fucking *wild* as Bhodi sinks lower, his lips skimming my abdomen.

I swear. A lot. In French.

Then I come, shaking with the force of it, and if I wasn't certain before that no one else on earth will ever make me feel like this, I am now.

Destroyed, I come down, shivering as Bhodi slows his wicked mouth and pulls off me.

He can't hide his grin. Doesn't even try. "Better?"

"Better than what?"

He brings us level again and taps my temple. "Than whatever was going on in there."

I can't remember what thoughts feel like. I make an unintelligible noise and think I might die here on this rug.

Then I feel him, still rigid and hotter than my seared nerves, and I get a second wind. "Come here."

An order. A plea.

Both.

Doesn't matter. Bhodi hears me and he brings his cock to my mouth.

He's so hard. And he's big too—not that it matters. I like everything. I like *him*, and taking him down my throat is the kind of perfection we're born for. And the sound he makes? The groan I've been hanging on for this whole fucking time?

It spears through me, etching on my brain forever, and the only thing better than that is making him groan *again*.

We've worked each other up so much that it doesn't take long for Bhodi's legs to tremble. I bite him, testing him, and he throws his head back, arching his spine, rooting his hands to the rug to keep himself upright. "Fuck. Tam."

One day. That *when* from earlier, it means something, and

the voice in my head that wants to argue is a distant thing I don't care about. I bring Bhodi to the edge, tempted to draw it out, but seeing him come is life, and I can't hold back. I give it everything. He shatters, and it's all I've ever craved from giving pleasure to someone else.

It really is fucking perfect, and so is the world we return to as we come up for air. The low light of the room. The quiet crackle of the logs in the burner. The scent of woodsmoke and sex heavy in the air.

Bhodi flops beside me, still breathing hard. There's an inch between us and I don't like it. "Lie with me?"

He edges closer, setting his chin on my chest. "You warm enough?"

I'm scorched earth, inside and out, and I need him closer still. I tug him until he's wrapped around me and it still doesn't feel enough. "I don't think I could ever be cold with you around."

Fourteen

BHODI

I wake up on the rug. The fire's still going. There's a pillow beneath my head and the sheets tucked around me. But I'm alone, and anxiety seizes my chest before I even crack an eye.

He left.

I sit up, bringing a hand to my chest, as if I can slow the pace of my heart with my palm. But I can't. The only distraction I have is the raucous bark coming from outside, and the realisation it's already growing light.

Rudy.

Of course it is. He barks like no dog I've ever known. High-pitched and *angry*, even when he's happy. Loud, first thing in the morning. Tam's neighbours must love him.

You love—

Fuck.

No.

I scramble from the floor and stagger to the windows that are now concealed by blinds I didn't know existed until last night. Until Tam came over and shut them so we could get naked without giving his brother an eyeful.

If that's why he came over.

If it even matters.

At the last second, I remember to drag on some sweats before rolling up the blinds. Then I'm greeted by another picture-perfect day on Stardust Lane. Clear skies and trees heavy with snow, swaying in the kind of wind that turns your cheeks pink.

It's a scene that demands pin-drop silence, but no one gave Rudy the memo. Or Tam as his deep voice rumbles an expletive I don't catch through the glass.

I wish I could see him, but the fence divides us. I can see the upper floor of his house, and I know he's not there, so I don't bother looking. Instead I stand and listen to his noisy start to the day, forcing logic into my brain. He left because he has responsibilities. A dog, a job. A brother who needs him more than I do.

Can't pretend it's not jarring to wake up with nothing but the ghost of him left on my skin, though. It's too familiar, and I don't like it. It makes me want to go back to bed and pretend the day hasn't started yet. Shame the universe has other plans for me in the form of the shrill beep of my phone.

I know that beep. It's the alert tone I set for the hospital. Either I messed up on my last shift, or they need me in on my rest day to cover someone else's, and I'm not sure which is worse.

My phone is buried somewhere on the bed no one slept in last night. The beeping has stopped by the time I dig it out, but Marla has left me a message that sends me trudging into the shower for a twelve-hour day shift.

It's then that I notice the cursive script on my arm.

The numbers about to smudge and run beneath the hot spray.

"Shit." I jerk away so fast I nearly brain myself on the tiles, and dash across the annex to where I've left my phone.

I type in the number and save it under *Tam*. Because it has to be, right? Unless a stranger crept in after he'd gone and graffitied my skin. But that would mean two people exist who write with the flair and beauty Tam does, and I refuse to believe that's true.

Dazed, I drift back to the shower.

Tam's handiwork washes away and I miss it. I stare at my arm as if the digits are embedded in my flesh, but alas, once they're gone they leave nothing but blank skin in their wake, and I regret reacting to my phone and signing up for a shift I want to work as much as I want to stick my head in the oven.

Time isn't on my side.

I get ready at record speed, thankful Tam installed a washer-dryer in the annex and the scrubs I dumped in there *last week* are good to go. And that at some point between him leaving me naked on the rug and me waking up, he's scraped my car free of ice and drawn a message on the back windshield.

Drive slow.

The two swirly words are another piece of art I can't keep, and I wonder if it's fate trying to tell me what I already know. That however into me Tam was last night, it's temporary. He doesn't do relationships, and while I might've made an exception for him—or I will if we ever get that far, he's not going to make one for me.

No strings. Why can't you just enjoy that for once?

Heh. Maybe I can. And for him, I'll try. I have to. I already know if he comes knocking again it's beyond me to turn him away. I haven't come like that in as long as I can remember. I get hard just thinking about it. While I'm *driving*. Which is awesome—insert sarcasm—since Tam's cute gesture means I'm pulling up at the hospital in no time at all.

I've been called in because HDU and ICU are chock-a-block with the survivors of a fire on a city industrial estate. The hospital is filled with police and soot-covered firefighters, a sight that warns me the day to come is going to be long and busy, so I take a moment to open WhatsApp and thumb out a message.

> Bhodi: please tell me this is you

The message blasts into the ether and the ticks turn blue before my eyes.

> Tam: depends who you are

I can't tell if he's serious or flirting, but I don't have time to find out. I type out most of what's on my mind and fire it back.

> Bhodi: it's Bhodi. thanks for last night
> —for trusting me. it was amazing and
> just what I needed xx

That's it. All I can say. And maybe it's too much, but I don't have the kind of job that makes room for distractions. I pocket my phone before Tam can reply and boot him from my mind.

I'm a different version of myself when it's this busy at work. On HDU, I barely think about Tam. Then I get bumped to ICU and I don't think about him at all. I'm consumed with keeping my patient alive and I do it with a singular focus.

It's not the easiest distraction technique out there. But it works, and there's something about pressing your hands to a man's chest to keep his heart pumping that puts things in perspective.

I'm not going to die if Tam doesn't want to swap blowjobs again.

Or if he blanks me.

Ghosts me.

Life is worth more than sex, and so am I.

I'm on my way back to my phone to test how married to that theory I really am. It's evening now, and the fraught atmosphere of a major incident has eased. Crackly Christmas music plays in the lift and the whole hospital is covered in festive artwork drawn by kids. I'm hungry. And tired. I want that fire back in the log burner and Tam's arms around me again, but I'll settle for another shower, a plate of hot food, and maybe, just maybe, a text message that doesn't make me feel like warmed up shit.

"Hey."

I spin around in an empty corridor. A firefighter stands behind me. He's in plain clothes, but I recognise him from this morning, because he's massive. Like, the tallest human I've ever met in real life. He's worried, though, *still*, and for the first time today, I can do something about it. "Your friend's doing well. I just took him to the main ward."

"I know." The firefighter gives me a half smile that does nothing to lighten his face. "I wanted to say thanks for everything you did for him. I don't know what we'd have done if anything happened to Galen."

I nod. "You're welcome. Did you get your shoulder looked at?"

"Nah. It's fine."

The way he shrugs it off is familiar, and it makes sense that the firefighter's disregard for his own wellbeing reminds me of Tam, but it's not that. "Did you ever work in Cornwall?"

The firefighter blinks. "No."

"Oh. Well you must have a doppelgänger down there somewhere. I swear I've met someone who looks just like you."

It's an awkward way to end a conversation, but the firefighter has other places to be, and so do I. He shrugs again and walks off. I continue to the break room and finally lay eyes on my phone.

I'm prepared for a blank screen. For that wall of silence.

But Tam's right there waiting for me.

> Tam: you were everything I needed too

> Tam: if it's a one-time thing for you, that's cool. nothing will ever be awkward, i promise. but...i really want to see you again xx

My heart skips. Tam doesn't look like the kind of man who punctuates texts with kisses, but I'm the kind of man who likes it. And as for the rest of it...I want to see him again too, and maybe that dream of a fire and his warm arms isn't as distant as it felt when I woke up alone this morning.

It's just sex.

So?

Sex can be warm and comforting. It can be anything we both want it to be. And Tam...he's my friend. We can make this work. I know we can.

I drive home with that mantra playing on a loop in my head. It's dark already, more frost on the roads. Black ice that almost makes me think of Tam lying on a hospital bed with a faceless nurse pounding his chest. But despite the crazy day I've had, I feel good, and it lasts until I get home to find Tam's van gone.

Yawning, I haul myself out of the car and shuffle past his front gate in a daze. His front door rips open and I jump out of my skin.

"Bordel de merde!" A man appears and thrusts Rudy out, brandishing him like a lion cub, turning him this way and that. "There's no one fucking out here. Stop barking at your own farts."

By the French cursing, I can only assume it's Tam's brother. And as he rotates back to the door, his dark hair and olive skin confirms it.

The knowing mischief in his gaze as it lands on me is different, though. "You're the hot lodger."

"Tenant," I correct, leaning on the gate and scrubbing a hand through my hair.

"That what they're calling it these days?"

"Calling what?"

"The daft grin you've put on my moody brother's face all day."

"Tam's not moody."

Sab grunts. "Give it time. You got plans tonight?"

"Uh. No."

"Good. Come and have dinner with us."

Sab spins and ambles into the house like it's a done deal.

I hesitate. I know the aroma filtering from Tam's house. It's the meat and bean thing he cooks in a clay pot that's as warming

148

as he is, and I want it in my belly as much as I want Tam. But he's not here. And if he'd wanted to have dinner with me, he'd have said, right?

He hasn't any other time you've wound up eating together.

Because he couldn't. We hadn't swapped numbers. But things were different now. If he wanted—

"Come in and shut the damn door. This little rat is clawing the fuck out of me."

Sab's voice booms, making me jump all over again. I slip through the gate and into the house, shutting the door behind me.

I'm instantly hit by the scent of meat and garlic, and the heat of a log burner twice the size of the one in the annex, a scene I've walked into before. But the baby toys scattered around are new, and the Dubois brother waiting on me in the kitchen has shorter hair, broader shoulders, and a distinct lack of ink staining his fingers.

The way he moves around the kitchen is the same, though. "Who taught you to cook?"

Sab glances up from the walnuts he's shelling for what I've come to learn is Tam's favourite salad. "Aunty Maron. She's a big believer in child labour in the kitchen. And she's a childhood nutritionist, so we got all the good stuff when we went to her place every summer."

"How did Tam end up a sugar nut then?"

"Dubois boys have addict genes. He got lucky with his vice."

No resentment colours Sab's tone. But he opens the fridge anyway, concealing his face for a moment, leaving me to hover by the counter, one eye still on the front door.

I don't know if I'm waiting on Tam or planning an escape,

and the dilemma messes with my head. I want to be here, but what if Tam doesn't feel the same? What if his hookup from last night is the last person he wants to see when he comes home?

"Mon pote, take your coat off." Sab's mixed dialect throws me. "Take your coat off," he repeats. "Tam keeps this place like a furnace."

I haven't noticed, too distracted by everything Tam to pay much attention to my surroundings. But I take my coat off anyway and hang it on the hook, leaving my shoes at the door, knowing Tam will see them before he sees me—*warning* him that I'm here.

"Are you always this quiet?"

"Hmm?"

Sab leans his elbows on the counter, watching me drift back into the kitchen. "My brother doesn't make you sound like the quiet type."

"I'm not quiet."

"Long day?"

"Yeah. Unexpected too, I was supposed to be off."

"I know how that goes." Sab slides a beer in front of me. "Not sure my job is as important as yours."

"You do something with wood, right? Like the worktops that fell on Tam?"

"That's what happened to his wrist?"

"He didn't tell you?"

Sab scowls. "He said he knocked it about a bit in the garage."

"That's true, I suppose."

Sab rolls his eyes to the ceiling, muttering something French, and it's so like Tam that my heart aches with longing.

For my landlord. My *friend*. And the dude who sucked me dry last night before I zonked out on him.

"If it's any consolation, I think it's healing okay."

"You *think*?"

"I don't have X-ray vision, but it's following the trajectory I'd expect for a healing fracture."

Sab absorbs this, picking at the label on his beer bottle. "I still can't believe you got him to go into the hospital. He wouldn't drive by that place for years after the crash."

"I didn't get him to do anything. He made the decision himself."

"Merde. You really are good for him."

I don't know what to say to that, but I'm saved by a squawk from the baby monitor by the stove.

Sab disappears upstairs. It leaves me alone in the ground floor of Tam's cosy house, and I take a moment to glance around without his biblical hotness to occupy me. The wood floors and squishy couch are already seared in my memory, but I see other things now—family snaps I haven't seen up close, pens—*so many* pens—and a photograph of a bike.

I wonder if it's the one he crashed, but contemplating that takes me back to how I felt when I thought about him in ICU, and I can't handle any more of that today.

"You're standing where I put the Christmas tree."

For the second time tonight, I startle like a newborn deer, and spin around to find a Dubois brother clutching a tiny dog. But it's the right brother this time—it's *Tam*—and he has frost flakes in his shaggy dark hair. "You want me to move?"

Tam stares, like he's drinking me in. "Only if I get to come with you."

It's in this moment that I know, for tonight at least,

everything is okay. The way he looks at me, the way his voice wraps around those words. The zero hesitance in the single long stride he takes to erase the distance between us. There's no room for doubt and I've run out of the will to search for it.

Tam sets Rudy down and draws me into a hug. "How did I get lucky enough for my dinner to be cooked *and* you're in my house already?"

I return his embrace, fighting with all I have not to sink into his arms and never come out. "Sab caught me outside and dragged me in. He asked me to stay for dinner, but you don't have to—"

Tam kisses me. Like, *really* kisses me, stealing whatever breath he hasn't already claimed with his frosty hair and big hug. "Bhodi, you being here to have dinner with me is the stuff of my fucking dreams. I've been thinking about you all day."

I can't lie and tell him I've been thinking about him all day too. But then, maybe things don't have to be literal to be true. The firefighter who nearly died from smoke inhalation. I wasn't thinking of Tam when we brought him back from a crash. Or when he opened his eyes and laughed at his stressed friends. But I felt...*something* I might not have done if I'd never met Tam. "There's nowhere else I'd rather be right now."

Tam grins.

He's so beautiful.

I kiss him again, he kisses me back, and we sway from the force of it. Of how good it feels to live in this moment and not think of the past or the future. Maybe it's the answer I've been searching for my whole life.

Or maybe I've been searching for Tam.

The thought intrudes on the peace I find in his lush mouth.

The kiss stutters and I pull back as Sab clears his throat from somewhere behind us.

"Get a room."

Tam ignores him till he spots the dark-haired, dark-eyed baby on Sab's hip and his expression lights to one I've never seen. "Ma chérie. Why are you awake?"

Sab gives him a droll look. "All the snogging woke her up."

"Ta gueule." Tam takes the baby and glares at his brother.

Sab just grins and slides back to the stove, and it doesn't take long for Tam's features to soften again.

He spins the baby in a slow circle. Then he crosses the room to an old chest and opens a drawer, rummaging around until he finds a board book that's unlike anything I've seen on the paeds ward.

Even from where I still stand by the photo of the motorbike, I can see how beautiful this book is, each page etched with the style of writing I am, by now, as familiar with as I am Tam's lips.

I venture a little closer. "You made this, didn't you?"

He nods, eyes on the baby. "For Esme. Give her something to do when her dad won't stop talking."

I don't need a translator to understand the growl that emanates from the kitchen. I laugh. The baby—Esme—does too, and Tam's smile?

My god. I'm in so much trouble.

The book is written in French. Tam settles on the couch and reads it to her while I watch, trying not to feel as though I'm intruding on an intimate family moment. But it's as easy as it is entrancing to see how much he loves that baby. How much Sab loves the pair of them as he peeps at them from the kitchen.

Esme eventually falls asleep on her uncle.

He takes her back to bed and we eat the meal Sab's cooked at the kitchen counter.

It's livelier than the dinners Tam and I have shared before. Sab's exhausted by the turn his life has taken in recent days, but he's chatty too, as if the quiet Tam often prefers gets under his skin, and he doesn't seem to know what to do with himself when the evening draws to a close.

"You should go to *bed*." Tam all but pushes him towards the stairs. "I swear you've been awake for three days straight."

Sab slips me a smirk. "Is he trying to get rid of me?"

"Not on my account." I'm already in the hallway, stepping into my shoes and rescuing the bag I abandoned by the door. "But he's probably right about you needing some rest."

Sab grunts and I take my cue, leaving the Dubois brothers to figure it out themselves.

I step out of Tam's house and face the frigid night air. Sab's right about Tam's place being a furnace, and I'm unprepared for the bitter wind that blasts me as I head for the annex with my coat unzipped and flapping in the winter gale.

The shower calls my name. I seek sanctuary in the blast of hot water and steam, then I remember the ball of scrubs in my car that need to come in and be washed. Getting cold all over again holds little appeal, but I've let adulting slip recently and I need to step up.

I make the mad dash in the wind and hurry back to the annex, already resenting the six seconds it's going to take me to load the washing machine.

"Bhodi!"

I spin around to find Tam jogging after me. For once he has shoes on, but his hair is as damp as mine, and there's a wildness in him that I feel to my core. "What's wrong?"

Tam reaches me, not hesitating before he draws me in, sliding his big, warm hands along my jaw. "I was going to ask you the same thing."

"What do you mean?"

"You didn't have to leave."

"It's late."

"That's not why you scarpered."

"Sab needs you."

"Sab needs to sleep."

"What about you?" His lips are too tempting. I steal a kiss. "What do you need?"

Tam takes a slow breath. I see the conflict rage in his complex brain before he floors me with the truth. "I need *you*."

Fifteen

BHODI

I need you.

I don't stop to consider what that means. What it *could* mean.

Or what it doesn't.

I seize the moment. I take Tam by his good hand and lead him to the annex.

Fumble the keys.

Drag him inside.

Not that he takes much dragging, until I remember that he likes it—to give himself up to the moment. To *choose* it after he spent so long with no choices at all.

I kick the door shut and shove Tam against it. In the dark, his eyes gleam, as feral as I suddenly feel, and I know he didn't come here for a chat.

I'm too worked up to worry that he only wants me for sex. To disregard every non-sexual encounter we've shared and what they might mean. I have the rest of my life to overthink all that. Right now, I *want* him, and everything that comes with it. "I want to fuck you."

Tam bites my bottom lip. "I've been dreaming about you saying that to me."

"Good dreams?"

"The fucking best."

"Don't get your hopes up." I tug him from the door and relieve him of his faded tee in one fluid movement. "I haven't topped in...I don't even know. It might be terrible."

"You said that about blowjobs and I barely survived."

"Yeah?"

Tam pushes my coat from my shoulders and wrenches my shirt over my head. "Yeah."

They're the last words we exchange for a while. Getting naked becomes our priority, and then we fall onto the bed I haven't slept in since he lay in it with me last night.

Hot skin and rumpled sheets.

It's the perfect combination, and by now we've kissed so many times it's as easy as breathing. So natural even Tam's cock, hard against my abdomen, feels dangerously like coming home.

I'm scared of that feeling and I'm not so kiss-drunk on him that I don't know it. To need the oblivion of sliding down his body, hooking my arm around his hip and devouring his dick with my mouth.

Tam groans, deep and violent. "Fuck."

Yeah. We're gonna. But I want this first, and not just because there's a devil in my head whispering that my lapsed topping skills are going to come up short. I want it because it's magic to watch Tam's composure slip. To *feel* it. He's so expressive I can't look away, even with him crammed down my throat, and when this is over and our lives have both moved on, I know this is what I'll remember.

"Bhodi." Tam gravels my name and digs his fingers into my shoulders. "Sois doux avec moi—I don't wanna come yet."

I have no idea what the first part of that sentence means, but I hear the plea in the second and release him from my mouth.

Tam's breathing hard.

So am I.

But we're just getting started.

Reading his gaze, I walk on my knees and tap his lips with my cock. He grins and flicks his tongue over it, and it's my turn to lose my mind as his hot breath heats my skin.

I'm going to fuck him.

It's a certainty now—as if it was ever in doubt—but first, he wants my dick in his mouth and I'm gonna give him what he needs.

Tam sucks cock like he does everything else. Like *art*, even as I let him goad me into screwing his mouth. Fucking his tight throat. An ache builds in my belly, the muscles in my thighs bound taut enough to snap. Only the thought of swapping this to being buried inside him stops me blowing my load too early.

Yeah, that's right. I don't want to come yet either.

It's how I find the strength to drag my dick from his wet and swollen lips, and leave him on the bed while I find a bag I haven't even thought about unpacking yet.

Condoms.

Lube.

I'd left them buried as a reminder to think before I dive head-first into something else that will ultimately hurt me. But

I'm not thinking right now, and if I were, I'd tell myself that my eyes are wide open this time. I know who Tam is. What he wants.

No strings sex.

I can do this.

I *want* this.

I go back to the bed. Tam is waiting, his face limned by the soft glow of the lamp I turned on when I came home, his hard dick wrapped in his tattooed fist.

Damn.

More blood rushes south, spinning my head, as he stares at me as if we do this all the time. As if he's a regular fixture in my bed and what happens next is inevitable.

Inevitable.

That word.

It's relevant. But I don't stop to puzzle it out. Without putting voice to how I'm feeling, I roll on the condom and reach for Tam, tugging him down the bed to where I want him.

Where I *need* him.

Closer.

More.

All of it.

Despite his injuries, Tam is lithe and flexible. He hooks me in with his legs, guiding me to where he wants me most, and I'm gentle as I align us.

He wants it rough—

No.

That's not what he said, and in this moment, I'm more aware of it than ever. "Ready?"

Tam licks his bottom lip. "What do you think?"

"I think I'm going to fuck my dick inside you and you're going to tell me if you need me to stop, okay?"

"Okay, Bhodi."

I push forward, breaching him, rapt as his nose flares with desire and his jaw unhinges more and more with every slow slide of my cock. And honestly, I get it. I know how it feels to take a man inside my body. That burn. That rush. The flood of emotion that comes even with a stranger.

Or maybe that's just me.

Either way, we're not strangers, and we haven't been since that night in the hospital car park, when a deeper part of me had known that our brief encounter was just the start.

I'm all the way in. With Tam's legs still wrapped around me, we're closer than close. I lean down to kiss him, parting his lips with my tongue, gliding it against his, swallowing the rough noise that escapes his throat, trapping his dick with my abs. My soul aches to rock forward, but I hold back, enjoying the moment before he breaks the kiss early and flexes his hips.

"Fuck me, Bhodi."

For a long second, I gaze at him, absorbing how tight he is, and how hard I'll have to fight to stave off the eye-rolling pleasure of giving him what he wants. But I know it's a fight that whatever happens, I can't lose. So I do what he does—what he chose all those years ago—and let it all go.

I fuck him. And I'm not gentle.

It isn't quiet either. Tam tells me what he wants, and I give it to him, and every sound he makes goads me into fucking him *harder*.

We cover every inch of the bed.

And then I put him on his knees.

Exertion works Tam's lungs.

He drops his head, taking a moment. I find myself at one with the scars on his back, some vast, some small, but each one a map of the man who, despite my best intentions, has consumed me so entirely since we met.

Leaning down, I trace one with my tongue.

Tam shivers. "Bhodi."

It's all he says, but I hear him. Still inside him, my lips to his spine, I start to move again, punching my hips to the rhythm I've already learned makes him set his jaw and *moan*. The rhythm that drags me into a heady trance where there's nothing but tight heat and the slap of skin on skin. It's perilous. That coil in my belly is a snake, waiting to strike. But it's so good I can't stop, and I fuck Tam like this for what feels like hours. Until my lungs start to burn and his legs tremble.

Until there's nothing left for us but the end.

I drag Tam upright. His strong arm goes around my neck and he arches his back.

Digging a knee into the mattress, I double down, grinding it out, chasing his climax more than my own, and I get my reward in his gritted out French expletives. In the hallowed way his deep voice wraps around my name. Tam detonates, and it's as beautiful as he is. A holy thing that catapults me off the edge, and we come together in a mind-blowing haze of the sweetest high.

I've never felt anything like it. Only the fact I'm still inside Tam, and I've put him through a marathon of hard sex, stops me collapsing on the ruined bed and sleeping forever.

We're both wrecked.

I ease out of him and stagger to the bathroom, grateful that every facet of the annex is within a few steps. I dump the condom, grab a towel, and go back to Tam to help him clean up.

Then we lie together in the dark, just breathing, until his hands find mine and he squeezes my fingers as hard as I fucked him.

I squeeze him back. "Okay?"

Tam takes a slow and shaky breath. "Yeah, baby. I'm okay."

Sixteen

TAM

I lie to Bhodi. I'm not okay. I called him *baby*, and it wasn't a mistake.

It's how I feel as I drift to sleep beside him for the second night running, and when I wake with my arms around him and my face pressed between his shoulder-blades. It's how I feel when I realise he's still sleeping and he's more beautiful now than he's ever been.

That's quite the fucking claim, but with Bhodi it's always been more than how he looks, even if he's so pretty right now I might legitimately die from it.

It's the contentment in my heart as I stare at him. The peace. And the sadness that comes from knowing I have to wake him.

Don't sneak out on him. Learned that lesson yesterday when he gazed at me like he was so fucking certain I never wanted to see him again.

"Bhodi." I kiss his neck on a whisper. "*Bhodi*. Wake up."

Bhodi breathes a little deeper. Then his eyes flash open. "What is it? Are you okay?"

I stop him bolting upright and kiss his neck again. "Sab's heading out this morning. I need to be there, but I can't leave without saying goodbye."

A beat passes before Bhodi relaxes, and the readiness in his jewel gaze softens a little. "Is he coming back?"

"I have no fucking idea. I just need to make sure he knows he can."

Bhodi nods, understanding, even as his gaze dips. "See you later...maybe?"

"There's no fucking maybe about it." I breathe him in one last time. Then I get up, throw my clothes on, and leave without looking back, because I know one glance, however fleeting, will burn my resolve to the ground.

Merde, I'm not built for how hard it is to walk away from him when I know he needs me to stay. But Sab...he's my brother. I can't let him go without telling him, even though he already knows, that my home is his home for as long as he needs it to be.

At least, that's my intention. Then I walk into my house to Rudy's apocalyptic barking and Sab's smug face and I feel like chucking a bucket of water over the pair of them.

"Don't." I jab a finger at him with one hand while I stuff a toothbrush in my mouth with the other. "Don't say a fucking word."

Sab threads his arms across his chest. "Why? You want privacy?"

"It's not that much to ask."

"Then shut the blinds when you get banged, bro. I'm scarred for life over here."

I don't blink. I don't breathe. "What?"

Sab comes closer and pokes my bicep hard enough to make me sway on my feet. "The blinds in the annex. I got the not-shock of my fucking life when I got up for a piss last night."

"Not-shock?"

"Oui-oui. I mean, it wasn't like I didn't know you went over there to get some. Just didn't expect to find a front row seat on the landing."

"I didn't go over there to *get some*." I ignore the rest of it. I have to, or I really will throw something at him. "It's not about that."

"What is it about then? And don't tell me you're just friends. You could power every Christmas light in the world from the chemistry between you."

Sab's question throws me. I have no answer for him and it spins my head that I can't figure it out. That the roadblock in my brain is still standing, even after the nights I've spent with the nicest bloke I've ever met. "Leave me alone."

"All right."

Sab steps away and starts gathering his things. Esme plays on the rug in front of the guarded log-burner Sab's already lit, and away from his inquisition, I smell the breakfast I know he's cooked and left in the oven for me.

I ditch my toothbrush and scoop Esme from the rug, straightening the hat on her tiny head. She regards me with a deep Dubois gaze just like her dad's, but she has no answers for me either, and it dawns on me that I have to let them both go.

"What are you going to do when you get home?" I trail Sab outside with Esme in my arms. "Where are you going to sleep?"

"On the fucking driveway if I have to."

"Sab."

"What?" He takes Esme from me and straps her into her seat. "What do you want me to do? Live with Charmaine and her fuckboy? Or leave my baby there and piss off to a hotel?"

"I want you to be safe. Both of you."

"We will be."

I'm unconvinced enough that I feel like following him home to Manchester, but I know I can't. Charmaine dislikes me at the best of times, and this is the worst. "Don't do anything stupid."

"Like what?"

"Like letting her goad you into fucking shit up."

Sab shuts Esme in the van and straightens to face me. "I'm not going to do that, I promise."

"I love you."

"I know." We hug. "I love you too. That's why I need you to take that breakfast I made you down the garden and let yourself have something nice for once. Give me one less thing to worry about, eh?"

He leaves on that note. I watch him drive away with a lump in my throat, but it's an affliction I'll have to live with until I see him again.

The van disappears. I wait until I can't hear the engine anymore, then I slowly spin round and find myself face-to-face with the one soul on this earth who can soothe the worry building in my heart for my brother.

Bhodi stands behind me, dressed in the gym clothes he wears for running, bottom lip caught between his teeth. "Hey."

I don't hesitate. I step to him and rescue that lip, claiming it for myself. I kiss him as if we haven't already parted ways this morning. As if we're still rolling around on his bed like we did last night. "Are you heading out to get all sweaty without me?"

Bhodi hums against my mouth. "It's good for me—to run off some steam. I get in my head if I don't do it often enough."

"I used to burn around on my hog for the same reason."

"Your what?"

"My bike. I liked to ride fast, but it got me in the end."

"Don't talk about that like it was your fault." Bhodi rubs his warm nose against mine before he pulls away. "It wasn't."

I know that. And I've known it for a long time, but watching Bhodi back up scrambles my brain. Wherever he's headed, and for whatever reason, I don't want him to go. I want him back in my arms, even more than I want him in bed, and it's a physical pain to stand here, still and silent, as he spins around and jogs away.

It's different to watching Sab and Esme leave.

The same, but *different*, and I feel heavy as I trudge inside to find Rudy and figure out what the fuck I'm doing with my life today. I have so much work to do. It's my busiest week of the year and I have so many deadlines I've forgotten them all. But my head—and my heart—is still with Bhodi, and it's hard to think about Christmas poems and whimsical greetings cards. Only the fact that the more I get done now, the more time I'll have for him later drives me upstairs without thinking about the breakfast Sab left for us.

I take a shower and realise my whole body aches. For once, it's a sweet pain, but it makes me miss Bhodi more, and at my desk, I find myself scanning the horizon for him instead of putting ink to paper.

He's gone *ages*. Long enough for worry to form a tight cage around my heart, binding my muscles enough that I start to make mistakes. I'm drowning in a sea of scrap paper by the time his blond head finally appears at the end of the road.

I abandon my desk as if the ink and parchment on it aren't what saved me six years ago. I burn down the stairs and charge out of the house. Sans boots, of course, but I don't feel the damp ground, or the puddle I stomp through. I feel nothing but angst until I lurch onto the pavement in front of Bhodi, forcing him to skid to a stop.

"Where the fuck did you run to?" I blurt before he can react. "The North fucking Pole?"

Bhodi pushes his hair back, face flushed like it was last night, his eyes bright with endorphins and exertion. "Huh?"

"You've been gone ages."

"Have I?"

"Yeah." I reach for him and pull him into my arms. "I thought you were gone forever."

Bhodi frowns.

I realise I've lapsed into French, but repeating myself feels like madness, so I kiss him instead. "I missed you."

He's still confused. As if he doesn't see a reality where that can possibly be true, and I hate the bloke that came before me a little bit more, even though I believe Bhodi when he says his ex did nothing bad. Merde, I hate everyone that's ever so much as breathed wrong around Bhodi.

I hate *myself* for not meeting him ten years ago.

"Do you have a fetish for wet feet?"

I have a fetish for him. And how he makes me feel. But that sounds weird, even in my head, so I grab his hand and hustle him into my house, keeping my wayward thoughts to myself. "Sab made us breakfast."

"Us?" Bhodi hovers by the counter.

I open the oven and face the dried-up meal Sab made a thousand hours ago. Kick it shut again. "He saw us together last night."

Bhodi's bewilderment deepens. Then his eyes widen. "Oh shit. The blinds. I'm so sorry."

"Don't be. I installed them. If anyone should remember to close them, it's me."

"How much did he see?"

"Enough to think we needed a hundred croissants to recover, but they're a bit fucked now. You want bacon?"

Bhodi stares, and I can't work out if he's just gassed from his run or genuinely surprised that he's been on my mind, and Sab's, since I left him at dawn.

I give him a minute, ditch another pair of ruined socks, and open the fridge. It says a lot about Sab's current mental state that I still have food. Lots of it. I drag out the works and chuck it all in pans.

I'm chopping mushrooms when Bhodi comes up behind me. "I need a shower."

"Okay."

"I won't be long."

He isn't, but it still feels like a fucking lifetime has passed by the time he comes back.

I slide him a breakfast plate, and this time he doesn't look at it, or me, like he's scared we're not real.

"Thanks."

"How far did you run?"

"This morning?"

A sarcastic reply bubbles up my throat. I swallow it down and wait.

Bhodi shrugs. "I don't know. I just keep going until I'm done."

"Sounds like sex."

"Sex with me?"

"That's the only sex on my mind right now."

Bhodi chews, a subtle smirk dancing in his features, but there's shyness too, an emotion I didn't get from him last night when he fucked the hell out of me.

I finish my breakfast and wait for him. When he's done, I take his plate and drop it in the dishwasher, hustling him away from the rest of it before he starts cleaning up. "I have to work, but I like it when you're with me. I'm distracted as fuck, but somehow I get more done."

Bhodi runs a hand through his damp hair. "All I did last time was stare at you."

"Yeah, well. I liked it."

"Really?"

"Really."

The stand-off is brief, but long enough to let me know he's still having trouble believing I want him around. Can't lie, it breaks my heart a bit. Even without the intense attraction we share, and the mind-blowing sex, Bhodi is the best company. He's sweet, funny, and kind. He's fucking *healing*, and I can't let him go.

Metaphorically.

Literally.

It's a struggle to bypass my bedroom and face my crowded desk again, but with Bhodi within arm's reach, anything feels possible.

I put the radio on. Cheesy Christmas songs fill the space, and later, as the sky darkens with an oncoming storm, the fairy lights from that long-ago Instagram post cast a glow that brings a contentment I haven't felt in years.

It's not the music.

It's not the lights, or Rudy snoring in his bed at my bare feet.

It's Bhodi chilling beside me, working his way through the writing books I dug out for him, his brow furrowed in a concentration that's so enchanting I have no defence against it reeling me in.

I set my pen down, midnight ink staining my fingers, and edge closer, taking a peek over his shoulder. "Well, look at that."

"Shh. I'll fuck it up."

I watch him glide the nib over the complex letter combination he's reached in the workbook. It's not perfect, but it's a world away from how he was writing when I met him. "Have you been practising?"

"Not like this." Bhodi finishes the combination with a flourish that makes him wince. "I've been trying to follow the rules at work, though, and I haven't got in trouble for my chicken-scratch notes all week."

"Maybe you should write like this at work. Give them something to think about."

"They'd think I'd been body-snatched." He turns the page and cringes harder. "I never realised how much I could hate the letter *S*."

"Why do you hate it?"

"I can't get it to flow until the next thing. Think I need more practice, but every time I see it, I freak out and turn the page."

"It's not about practice." I press up behind him and wrap the fingers of my good hand around his wrist, guiding him through the combination he's so afraid of. "It's about accepting things are how they are, and you can be okay with that. And maybe even one day, you'll find it's the easiest thing in the world."

I trace his pen over the letters again. Then I let him do it, but I don't let go of his wrist. If anything, my grip tightens and the space between us narrows to nothing.

It feels so good to hold him like this. To watch his face as he breaks concentration and tips his head to smile at me.

This isn't what friends do. It's something else. I know it and I don't want to push it away. I don't want to run from it, and merde, I have to kiss him. So I do, and it's deep and long, and I can barely breathe through the sweet force of it. That I'm hard —*so fucking hard*—for him seems secondary, and there's so much I need to say to him right now. So much he needs to hear before real life catches up with us and he leaves my arms thinking he's just a casual fuck to me.

You told him that's all you ever want—from anyone, not just him.

I did say that, and I'm an idiot. But as I open my mouth to say so, Bhodi's phone buzzes up a storm on the desk. "If that's your boss, tell her to go jump in the canal."

"It's not my boss." Bhodi licks my cheek, then wriggles out of my hold. "It's my mum. She wanted to see the annex. I'll be back, okay?"

He's gone in the blink of an eye, and he doesn't come back before it's time for me to head out on deliveries.

I get caught in traffic.

All of it.

Then my van gets a flat tyre and I have to change it by the side of the road in the fucking rain. Wet and cold, it puts me in a foul mood and it's late by the time I stomp home with the fury of a thousand gods in my veins. With the way the latter part of my day has panned out, I expect Bhodi's car to be gone. Him at work or whatever.

But he's not gone. He's sitting on my wall with a cup of tea and an outstretched hand. "Come home with me?"

I say yes in every language I know.

Seventeen

BHODI

We fuck every night I don't work for ten days straight. It's not planned or even co-ordinated, it just happens. We cross paths on the driveway and barely make it inside before we're naked and tumbling onto my bed.

I try not to think about why it's always my bed, and when Tam's naked beneath me, his gritted moans all I can hear, not thinking is easy. Whatever it is between us, in bed, on the rug—on the hardwood floor when we don't make it that far—it works, and it's so close to perfect I almost forget it's temporary.

"...I don't do relationships anymore. Or even hookups unless it's with someone I know for sure doesn't want anything else."

Heh. On my rest day, I tag along with him to buy his Christmas tree from the farm in the next village. We go in the afternoon when it's already getting dark, and on the way home, I notice a spinning glow at the summit of Firefly Hill. "What's that?"

Tam has a mini roll half stuffed in his mouth. He takes a

giant bite and eats it before he's fit to answer me. "That's the hot jewellery maker who lives up there. He's a fire dancer too."

"A fire dancer who lives on *Fire*fly Hill?"

Tam grins. "Yup."

"For real?"

"It gets worse. He's shacked up with a real life *fire*fighter too."

"That's almost as bad as having a star tattooed on your face and living on on *Star*dust Lane."

Tam scowls. Kinda.

I laugh and steal the remaining half of his cake from where it's dropped into his lap. It's delicious and it shouldn't be, but I don't care. I eat it anyway and drowse to the tinny Wham! filtering out of the van's radio, an unpredictable contraption that's as knackered as I am after staying up all day after a night shift. The sickly-sweet sugar and Tam's company are a good distraction, but a frayed feeling loiters, ready to strike if I don't go to bed—*to sleep*—soon.

We pull up outside Tam's house. He goes for the tree in the back of his van, ready to hoist it inside by himself, but I'm there before he gets his hands to it, sharing the load. Tam might think I haven't noticed that the wild sex we've been having has aggravated his back injury. But I have. Because I spend way too much time gazing at him, and I'm not even remotely sorry about it.

I know where the tree goes—by the motorcycle photograph I find myself transfixed by every time my gaze lands on it. "Do you miss it?"

Tam slides up behind me, not touching, just there, warm and solid. "The bike or the life?"

"All of it."

"That's a tough question."

I turn to face him. "Why?"

Tam gives me the same frown he's been giving me for days now. Like there's something he wants to say, but he doesn't quite know what. "It was a great life while I was living it, but it's killed and hurt people I care about. And it took me away from Sab too much. I might've caught him before he fell so far if I'd been around more."

"Bet he doesn't see it like that."

"He doesn't."

Tam's hands twitch, as if he's thinking about reaching for mine. At least that's what my brain imagines, and then lights on fire. Tam's super tactile with everyone. The more time I spend with him, the more I see it. He gave the postman a hug yesterday.

You're not special.

It's just sex.

Friends, remember?

I step away and move to the boxes Tam's stacked on the coffee table while Rudy tries to attack them from the floor. Decorations I persuaded him to let me retrieve from the attic for him after we fucked in the annex before first light this morning. "La Rochelle." I read the heart-shaped ornament. "Is that where your family's from?"

"No, it's where we used to go on holiday. My dad's family are Parisian."

It takes me a second to compute what that means. "Paris?"

Tam nods and reaches over my shoulder to take the ornament. "My mum's lot are Scottish, but she speaks better French than any of us."

He kisses the back of my neck, grabs another bauble, and

drifts back to the tree as if a full-body shiver didn't just wipe my brain clean of all thought. But I *know* he knows. Because I told him a few nights ago, when I was buried deep inside him, that his touch casts a spell on me. What can I say? Bomb sex makes me chatty. But I regret it. Opening my big mouth, not the sex. Spilling my feelings means acknowledging them, and I'm not ready to admit that fucking Tam was a wonderful and terrible mistake.

It's just sex.

Right.

"Bhodi."

"Hmm?"

"Come here." Tam holds out his hand—the casted one, the fibreglass dented and dinged. He doesn't look at me, because he knows I'll come. That I can't resist his addictive affection. He doesn't know how scared I'm becoming of the day when it's gone.

It's just sex.

I go to him and wrap my arms around him from behind, as if that gives me more control. And maybe that's how I've settled in to fucking him so easily. Because it's easier to believe he wants me for more when he hooks his legs around my waist and begs me to stay inside him. As he slides a casual hand over my hip *now* and shows me a handwritten decoration made of cardboard and clay.

It's cute. "Did you make this when you were little?"

"I was eighteen and drunk. See how bad my writing used to be?"

"When you were *drunk*."

"It was like that when I was sober too."

I bite my lip as he leans against me, his back to my chest,

every contact point sparking a heat in my blood that should be sated already, but isn't, and it's starting to feel like it won't ever be. That I could fuck Tam ten times a day and it will never be enough. "How did you get into art therapy?"

Tam takes a breath and slowly lets it out. Not quite a sigh, but close. "I had a lot of anxiety after the crash. I kept hearing all the alarms going off when my heart wasn't beating right, feeling those hands on my chest, people shouting at me to live. And I didn't have the road to escape to anymore when I could barely fucking walk."

"How long did it take to work?"

"It was a few months before I woke up without being catapulted into my day by a panic attack. Then a year went by and I was still doing it, and now it's as much a part of me as riding my hog ever was."

"And at least it's something you enjoy. I hate running."

Tam straightens. "You run when you're anxious?"

I nod and his stare intensifies, like he's trying to peel back layers I don't even know are there. For the first time ever, his attention makes me squirm, and I back away from it, returning to his boxes of baubles.

He lets me go and we decorate his tree in relative silence, save Rudy's snoring now he's grown bored with trying to maul everything.

We've been quiet before, mainly after sex until I pass out first, and it's never been awkward, but it feels heavy now, and I know it's me. That for once, my instincts are doing the right thing and warning me that this easy companionship is dangerous for my soft heart, and I need to step back before it blows up in my face again.

"Do you want to put Sab's plastic monstrosity in the annex?"

I'm crouched at the foot of the gorgeous fir Tam chose at the farm. From a few feet up where Rudy can't reach, he's decorated it in shades of gold and red, and a few pink things he says are for Esme. Even with the drunken baubles and the angry dog trying to savage every branch, it's classy and cool, leaving me to assume the tat left in the boxes belongs to someone else.

To Sab, maybe. "You don't think he'll want it?"

"Not this year." Tam eyes me as I rise, bringing us face to face again. "He's coming back here on Christmas Day, but he has to leave Esme behind."

My heart sinks, another warning that I'm way too invested in my landlord-slash-hook-up's family. In his *brother*, who's been nothing but nice to me. "Do you think they'll work out a fair custody split?"

"No."

"No?"

Tam's expression darkens. With the lights from the tree making his brown eyes gleam, he looks more like the biker he used to be. "It's going to be all or nothing. I just don't know which way it's going to go yet."

"Sab can't lose Esme. He's an amazing dad."

"I know, but Charmaine's petty. She'd take her just to win. Just like she'd give her up if she got a better offer than growing the fuck up, and it's fucking twisted that I have to pray for that for Esme, but it's all I can do."

It's a horrible thing to contemplate when we've spent all afternoon turning Tam's beautiful house into a Christmas grotto his niece might not get to see. There's Christmas songs on the radio again, but they grate on me now, like they're mocking us. "I'm sorry you have to go through that."

Tam starts to smile and reach for me. But something stops him. "What's wrong?"

"Wrong?"

"Yeah. I know you're tired, but this feels like something else."

"What does?"

"This." Tam gestures between us. "Have I pissed you off since this morning?"

A frown creases my forehead as my scratchy, sleep-deprived brain struggles to keep up. We banged this morning. Then he worked, and I caught up on the errands I've let slide while I've spent every spare moment fucking him on every available surface of the annex.

The annex he owns.

Because he's my landlord.

"You haven't pissed me off."

"Then what is it?"

"I don't know." I rough a hand through my hair. "It's just—"

Just what? You're friends that fuck. He never promised you anything else. Just like Skylar, and everyone before him.

"Fuck." I want to punch something, and it's a feeling I'm not familiar with, like my words snarling up in my throat. I'm good at talking if people give me the chance. I'm good at *breathing*, but apparently, in this moment, I've forgotten how.

"Bhodi." Tam utters my name like it's the last word he'll ever say, and it's too much.

I reel away from him.

Hurt flashes in his gaze, instant and raw. "Hey." He holds

his hands up. "Whatever it is, you can tell me, okay? We're friends."

I laugh, I can't help it.

Tam's confusion deepens and the discord that springs up between us is so visceral Rudy lifts his head, disturbed by a soundless struggle neither of us truly understands.

"All right." Tam's voice pitches lower as he tries again to reach me. "Merde, let's fucking rewind."

"To where?"

"To wherever you need to be to calm the fuck down."

Calm the fuck down. I've had those words thrown at me before. Not Skylar, someone else. Someone insignificant, but maybe not as Tam's well-meant words trigger my frustration so hard I really do want to thump something. Probably myself, because if we're rewinding, perhaps it needs to be to the moment I found out the dude I'd accosted in the hospital car park was my landlord. When I had every chance to back off and find somewhere else to live.

Or find a new job.

A new town.

A do-over before my fresh start had even begun.

But no. I hooked up with the hot dude from the car park. I caught feelings for him, and now here we are, blazing heartache at each other under the light of a tree as beautiful as he is.

At least, my heart aches. Tam still looks confused, and that's my fault too. I'm giving him nothing. "I've really fucked this up."

Tam lowers his hands. "Fucked what up?"

"This." I snatch a breath that goes nowhere. "I thought I could do it, but I just fucking can't."

Tam solidifies, for the most fleeting moment. But it's the

escape I need and I back up again, needing out before I say something I can't take back.

Like fucking him being a mistake.

Because it wasn't.

Not the way he's going to take it if I can't find a better way to explain myself, and that's not happening today. I know it like I know Tam's going to chase after me if I don't move faster.

"Bhodi, wait."

I'm too slow.

Tam weaves around me, blocking my path. "*Wait.*"

It's not in me to physically push him away. I stop and he grips my shoulders, his touch heavy and grounding, but he doesn't speak, and his bewildered silence is worse than if he shouted in my face, because I deserve it as much as I deserve to love someone without feeling like I'm begging for scraps in return.

Tam doesn't make you feel like that. And Skylar didn't either. You made that mess all by yourself.

I shrug away from Tam. "Sorry, I'm just tired and in my feelings. I need a nap and a reality check."

"A reality check?" Tam's still in my way. I'm wider than him, but somehow, he seems like a giant blocking a causeway. "Is this about us fucking?"

Is it?

My brain flashes back to this morning. It was still dark out as I pushed Tam onto my bed and nudged his legs apart. I've come to learn that Tam doesn't need—or want—much prep. That I can be inside him in as long as it takes me to shove our clothes aside and find some lube.

Too fast.

That's what I thought. But maybe my brain had been trying to tell me something else.

"It's not about that." I try to rub the tightness out of my chest. "And it's not you—it's me. I knew this was a bad idea before I even met you."

Tam frowns. "I—"

His phone rings.

Loudly, with the tone he has assigned to family.

Sab.

Or his parents.

Either way, whoever it is trumps the clusterfuck I've set in motion, and it's how it should be.

I take advantage of his distraction and slip past him.

Tam curses, torn between me and his phone. "Don't go. Please?"

I could scream. I bring both hands to my head, ploughing my fingers into my hair, battling the urge to rip it all out.

But I don't go.

I step into my shoes, then I stand, rigid, while Tam darts for his phone and hate myself even more as the call rings out before he reaches it.

He comes back, phone clutched in his tattooed fist. *Maman* lights up the screen, and I feel even worse. His parents don't call much.

"Bhodi." Tam drops his phone on a nearby shelf and grasps my wrists, tugging my hands from my hair. "Just take a breath, okay? Whatever it is, it can't be that bad."

I almost believe him. But he doesn't release my wrists. He strokes my pulse points with his thumbs, his cast brushing my skin, reminding me how we first met. How I knew even then that the skip in my heart I felt for him was dangerous. "I can't fuck you anymore."

"Okay." Tam's grip tightens. "But that's just sex. What's really bothering you?"

"Just sex..." He's right. Of course. But hearing him say it tears me up all over again. Because fucking him has nothing to do with the warmth blooming where he holds my wrists, or the way his cinnamon scent spins my head. Or the concern in his gaze my soft and stupid heart takes for something else.

Just sex.

Just. Sex.

But it's not just sex for me, and it never was. I liked him. I cared about him. And now I'm drowning in a potent mix of the two that feels a lot like love, and I'm the biggest fucking idiot that ever lived.

I wrench free of Tam's grasp.

He recoils as if I've slapped him and holds up his hands in surrender. "All right, all right. If you need space from me, take it."

"That's the point, though, isn't it?"

Frustration darkens Tam's features, his brows knitting together. "*What* is?"

I don't want space from you.

But I can't say it. I have nothing but a big fat knot of wordless anguish and his phone rings again before I can even begin to unpick it.

It's his dad this time.

Tam's gaze bounces between me and the screen and I give him the out he needs.

I leave, and dash outside into the sleety snow that's begun to fall while I've been holed up in Tam's fairytale house with him. The crispness in the air is gone and everything feels damp and sad, even me.

Especially me, and the empty annex does nothing to lift my mood.

I sit on the edge of the bed where I fucked Tam this morning. In the gloom, listening to the sleet turn to rain, washing the sparkle off the ground and the trees.

My phone buzzes.

I ignore it.

A little while later, comes a quiet knock at my door, and I know it's Tam. It can't be anyone else, and I ache for him something rotten.

But I ignore that too and sit alone in the dark until the sky turns from black to pearl grey with one question on my mind. How the hell did I let this happen to me again?

Eighteen

TAM

Knowing Bhodi's upset cuts deeper than any injury I've ever endured. I'll break my back a thousand times for him. I'll carve out my liver and offer it to God before I'll let anything hurt him.

You hurt him.

Did I? I go over and over it in my work-addled brain and I can't figure it out. All I know is everything was great. Then it wasn't—it *isn't*—and, fuck me, I miss him.

Simmer down, son. It's been twelve hours.

Twelve hours since Bhodi left my house and didn't come back. Since he blanked my text and didn't answer the door. And now I'm standing at my desk, staring at his closed blinds, and losing my fucking mind.

I need to sleep. Not just because I have a mountain of work to do and I can't see straight, but because I have to drive to Manchester tonight and help Sab move out of his house without punching Charmaine's new boyfriend—a tall ask, whether I've slept or not.

And I can't fucking sleep. I *can't*. Not without seeing Bhodi, and honestly, it scares me. I haven't been so locked-in to someone in years. If ever. I loved Grey, and he hurt me. But I never felt like this about him. Never felt as though a piece of me would die if he wasn't okay.

I glide my pen across the piece I'm working on, unseeing, uncaring. I make an unholy mess and have to scrap it, and it joins the pile of crumpled card at my feet.

Merde.

I crouch to gather them up and a wave of fatigue batters the shit out of me. I'm not as tough as Bhodi. I can pull an all-nighter with the best of them, but not without a daylight nanna nap, and I'm reaching my limit of endurance.

Work has to wait.

I step away from my desk and tramp downstairs with every intention of knocking on Bhodi's door first. But I sit on the couch for a minute and wake up three hours later to find Bhodi's gone.

Harassing him with texts feels wrong while the one I sent last night sits unread. So I take Sab's awful plastic Christmas tree and leave it on the annex porch. Then I drive to Manchester for the night, and in the morning, I boot Roidy Dwaine into a muddy puddle at the side of the road.

It's not my finest hour, but at least Sab didn't do it.

That's what I tell myself hours later when I'm finally on my way home to retrieve Rudy from the neighbour he stays with on the rare occasions I'm not home. I don't look at my phone. I drive with my mind whirring a hundred miles an hour, and by the time I trudge into my house with Rudy tucked under my arm, I'm at my limit for that too.

Bhodi's the best thing that's happened to me in a hell of a long time. If he's upset, I have to fix it. And I'm going to.

Unfortunately for me and my hard-won positive attitude, his car is still gone and I wish I'd stopped Sab flushing my last pack of cigarettes down the bog.

I wish I'd learned my lesson too about falling asleep on the couch. I lose another few hours to it and when I wake up, the tree I left on Bhodi's doorstep is no longer there, but there's no sign of his car. As if he's been and gone while I slept, and fucking *hell* why is everything so hard? Why can't I just love someone and that be it?

I'm pacing my kitchen as that thought completes and I come to an abrupt stop, my brain lit up again with the two things that've been my constant companions for weeks now.

Bhodi and *love*.

It should be a revelation, but it isn't. Because I already know I love Bhodi, I've just never spelled it out to myself in literal terms. And I've never told *him*, and that's the fucking epiphany.

I love Bhodi and he doesn't know it. He thinks we're just banging. Friends with benefits at best, and at worst, another entanglement that's going to stamp on his heart when the heat dies off. Except...this thing between us, it's not going to die off. It's gonna grow, like it has every day, every hour, every minute, since we first laid eyes on each other.

It's not just sex, and it never was.

More than that, I don't want it to be. I want Bhodi in my arms—I need that.

I need *him*.

And I need to tell him before he spends another second believing the way I look at him when he's fucking me is anything less than it is.

I *need* to tell him I love him.

It drives me out of the kitchen and in search of my phone.

I find it in the hallway, on the floor by my boots and it leads me to realise Bhodi's coat is still hanging on the hook. I reach for it, already halfway out the door in my mind before I remember he's not there. That wherever he is, he's probably fucking cold, and I hate that as much as I hate that I've messed this up so badly. That I didn't tell him from the start that our FWB arrangement was messing with my head too.

Reeling, I leave the coat where it is and retreat upstairs with my phone, giving the tranquilising couch a wide berth.

In the studio, I contemplate my desk. I'm so behind and all-nighters aren't a sustainable answer. But I struggle to care about Christmas cards and handwritten gifts. I swipe at my phone instead and get my reward in the form of a text that arrived three hours ago.

> Bhodi: sorry I've been a ballache. and i'm sorry about the other night. i love being friends with you and i don't want to lose that

An instant frown heavies my face. I feel his nerves in every word and I hate it.

> Tam: You're not going to lose that. Ever. You matter to me xx

It's not as late as the dark makes it feel, but I'm still surprised that Bhodi reads my message and starts typing back.

And typing.

And typing.

And typing.

He's scared to say how he feels.

I'm not, but I don't want to tell him I love him over text. So I wait and try to pull myself together enough to work. Force myself to pick up a pen and write, like I had to all those years ago when I'd have rather jumped off a motorway bridge.

I've come a long way since then. I know how to ground myself. How to breathe when my mental health reaches a fork in the road. And my work is as good for me as it's always been. I'm unaware how much time has passed when my phone finally lights up. Just that the stack of cards I need to burn through is less.

> Bhodi: thanks for saying that. you don't owe me anything. sorry i've made this so weird

I set my pen down and hold my phone with both hands, measuring my words when all I want to do is blast him with the reassurance and love I'm not sure he's ready for.

> Tam: It's not weird for friendships to get complicated. You haven't done anything wrong. Are you at work?

> Bhodi: yeah

> Tam: When do you finish?

> Bhodi: midnight

Midnight. I glance at the clock on the wall and the hour tells me two things: One, Bhodi must've left for work about ten minutes before I woke up. Two, that I have just enough time to finish this year's Christmas orders and deliver them before most people around here are in bed.

Fate works in mysterious ways. It's almost like she wants me to finish my work before I get to live the rest of my life.

Outrageous.

I text Bhodi back.

> Tam: I'll be up when you get home and
> I'd really love to see you. Whatever
> you're thinking, don't. Let's talk first...
> please? x

The message is sent and gone before I think to question it, and then I settle in to wait. Bhodi's at work. I'm aware he probably doesn't have his phone in his pocket, and it's an hour before he responds.

> Bhodi: you don't have to humour me.
> it's fine. everything's fine

Fuck that.

> Tam: I'm not humouring you. And
> nothing is fine until I get to tell you that
> to your face

Bhodi doesn't reply. Or read the message. But again, I let it go and focus on my work until he comes back online a while later.

By then, I've smashed through my orders and I'm climbing in the van to make the penultimate deliveries of the year. Bhodi still doesn't reply, but with a couple of hours to go until he comes home, I can live with that.

I make my rounds. Go home and put the finishing touches to the gifts I'll deliver tomorrow. Then I wait by the window with Rudy, tracking every sweep of light on the road outside. Every rumble of an engine and every daft skip in my heart as I crane my neck to look for Bhodi. I wait and wait and wait for him.

But he doesn't come home.

Nineteen

TAM

For all the calm I've fostered while I've worked the night away, it dissolves like salt in water when three a.m. rolls around and Bhodi's still not home.

Chill. He's worked late before.

Sound logic, but it's lost on me as irrational dread grips my heart and I pace my house like a lunatic.

Something's wrong.

I have zero evidence except the darkened annex and the empty spot on the pavement where Bhodi's car should be, but I'm so convinced it's true I barely last another hour before I'm dashing outside to my van.

Sans boots, of course, and the return of the frost is the shock I need to stop me in my tracks.

"Fuck." I press my fist to my chest and take a deep breath, utilising every tool I possess. But the fear in my heart remains and I do the only thing I can think of. I call Sab and garble at him before he's even awake, a messy torrent of French and English even he has trouble understanding.

"Whoa." His voice catches like he's swallowed glass. "What's wrong?"

I say it all again.

I think.

I fixate on the rustling at Sab's end as if it can drown out the panic rising in me. The raw feeling I haven't faced head-on in years. I can't remember the last time my little brother had to talk me down from the ledge.

Bet he can, though, and I let flashbacks pound my brain with every weak moment I've ever had. Because that's super helpful right now.

"Take a breath," Sab orders. More awake. "Then go back in your house and call Bhodi instead of me."

"What if he doesn't answer?"

"Then you'll know he's driving or working, and either fucking way, he'll be home soon."

He's right. I know he is. Bhodi's shifts have run over before. By longer than this. But with so much unsaid between us, everything feels different.

I feel different. "Je l'aime." *I love him.*

"I know."

"How?"

"Because I know *you*. And I've never seen you as content and happy as you are around him—" Sab yawns and runs out of words.

Guilt threatens the anxiety still gripping me. He's sleeping in a shitty Travelodge after packing his stuff into storage, and I want him here with me. With Esme. But it's not happening anytime soon—if ever—and I have to accept that. "I'm sorry I woke you up. Go back to sleep."

"Tell me you love me and promise you won't drive while you're this wired."

"I love you."

"*Tam*, promise me. Or I'm getting in the fucking van and driving down there."

"Ne le faites pas." *Don't.* That's the last thing I want. I fight the tide, hurling everything I have at it, and finally get a tenuous grip on myself. "I'm good, I swear I won't drive if I'm messy."

"Promise."

"I promise."

"I don't fucking believe you. Or I'd make you swear on my baby girl's life. But I'm gonna trust you like you've always trusted me. Now simmer the fuck down and wait for your man to come home."

Sab tells me he loves me and hangs up. I'm not naïve enough to believe he goes straight back to sleep, but I can't do anything about that. I need him and he needs me. It's how it is.

I heard him, though. I go back inside, change my wet socks, and contemplate my phone before I realise how dark it is in my house. Like, pitch black, even the stand-by light on the TV is out.

Power cut.

It happens round here all the time, especially in winter. But like everything, it seems ominous now, and I fight for the calm Sab's forced on me and call Bhodi.

No answer.

I call once more, then tap out a message with shaky fingers.

Tam: You're not home and I'm really
fucking worried. Let me know you're
okay?

Damn. I was going for something more subtle, but it has to do. I fire it off and sink onto the couch, bracing my elbows on my knees and folding my hands as much as I can with this stupid fucking cast.

The urge to saw it off sweeps over me.

Bhodi's disapproval stops me, and I hold onto that. To the fact he'll be home any minute and the spiked fear lancing my heart will be over.

This is you.

Not him.

I close my eyes, smelling woodsmoke from the burner and the piney scent of the Christmas tree. Breathing deep, slowing my thoughts with every cycle of air. And for a while it works, until Rudy makes me jump out of my skin, barking at something and fucking nothing, as restless by now as I am.

Calm deserts me. I surge to my feet and stride to the window in case I've somehow missed Bhodi coming home and slipping into the annex without talking to me. With every light out, he might've assumed I was sleeping.

Sound logic, but his car is still gone.

I call him again.

No answer.

Maybe the hospital lost power too and he had to stay.

Another theory that makes perfect sense, but the hospital is in the city, and in all the years I've lived here, the power cuts that affect the villages have never extended that far. *Natural disaster, then.* But that doesn't make me feel any better, and my phone is running low on battery.

Sab has my power banks. The only sensible thing I can think to do is to drive to the all-night petrol station and buy more. I make myself linger long enough to stamp into my boots, then I'm out the door and behind the wheel, gritting my teeth to keep my promise to Sab.

The streets are *dark*. Dawn is a couple hours off and I pass few vehicles. I pass the fucking *petrol station*, lit up by emergency lights, and I don't stop. I keep going, only realising where I'm heading when the hospital comes into view.

My foot falters on the accelerator and the van slows down. My concern for Bhodi is a noose throttling my windpipe, but old ghosts don't care about that. They smell disinfectant and blood. They hear the angry beep of machines, they hear Sab crying, and the panic monster waiting to strike finds some new friends.

Black spots dance in my vision and my hands tighten around the wheel. I'm not breathing right and I know better than to suck more air in. I let it out, slowly, and battle to keep the van moving. *You've been here twice recently and nothing fucking happened.*

Because of him.

No.

I know better than that too. With or without Bhodi, I'm stronger than the anxiety clawing at my back.

But fuck me, life is better with him.

I keep driving and rumble through the main entrance. Bhodi parks round the back, but I need a staff pass to get that far with the van. So I ditch it and hurdle the barrier on foot.

It's late and the car park is lit by a security light that's half broken. Shadows are everywhere and I decide that even when Bhodi's home in one piece, I hate him fucking parking here. *So what? You're going to tell him he can't? Or follow him to work every day like a fucking psycho?*

Considering it occupies my thoughts for the brief minutes it takes to search every inch of the staff car park, and then every space and bay beyond. I even check the side streets, but come up blank.

Bhodi isn't here.

He isn't fucking here.

I jog back to the van, my phone pressed to my ear, and I shout in frustration as my call goes unanswered, agitation flooding my veins again.

Bhodi, where are you?

I throw myself behind the wheel and leave the hospital car park with no real idea where I'm going, except that it's not my usual way home. The city slips by me in a blur, my body aching with wasted adrenaline, a headache squeezing my skull. Honest to God, I feel sick with fear, and it's so much worse than the PTSD that kicked the shit out of me after the crash.

Back then, I was afraid of something that had already happened. This is different—this is *real*, and if even a hint of my imagination is on point, I could lose Bhodi forever.

My phone buzzes with a message. It's on the seat and I can't see it while I'm driving.

Despite the madness raging in me, I pull over before I pick it up.

Bhodi.

Nope.

It's my brother and the caps lock on his smashed up iPhone is still broken from when he dropped it trying to stop me killing Charmaine's mope of a fuckboy.

Sab: FIND HIM?

198

Tam: No. I checked the hospital. He's
not there

Sab: DID THEY SAY WHEN HE LEFT?

I'm such a fucking idiot.

Tam: Didn't ask. I just looked in the
car park

Sab: WHAT IF HE DIDN'T DRIVE
THERE TODAY?

Tam: Then where the fuck is his car?

Sab: AT THE GARAGE. AT A MATE'S
HOUSE. THERE'S A MILLION
POSSIBILITIES BEFORE WHATEVER
YOU'RE THINKING

Tam: You don't know what I'm thinking

Sab: YOU THINK HE'S DEAD

Sab's not shouting at me on purpose, but it feels like he is, and the words stare up at me, stark and *loud*. I drop the phone on the seat and start driving again, longing for a cigarette so much that I search the glove box with my casted hand while steering with the other, and as luck would have it, I found a squashed box of the rancid Silk Cut I downgraded to when I was trying to quit.

No Zippo. But I jam a smoke between my lips anyway and wrestle with the van's corroded lighter. It barely gets warm, but somehow it's enough to light the cig and I take an inhale of toxic smoke that's a thousand times more kill than cure.

But it's something to do, and the familiarity of the ritual brings me back to earth. I'm heading for the motorway, I realise, a route I usually avoid like the plague, but I've never told Bhodi why, so I know he still drives this way to and from work, chugging along in his battered Golf with no clue that my blood is soaked into the slip road he takes to get there.

The slip road that's coming up ahead, but I don't give a single fuck about right now.

I drive on, smoking until the cig burns my fingers.

The slip road passes and I merge onto the motorway. There's zero traffic and the road starts to darken as I get nearer home and the power cut zone, and of course, the van stereo chooses the same eerie moment to crackle to life, blasting me with Bing Crosby at a volume loud enough to rattle my overwrought brain.

Wrestling with it derails me from smoking more, and with the comforting buzz of nicotine already at home in my nerves, my thoughts start to even out, common sense returning.

I just missed Bhodi. He's probably already home and wondering where the fuck *I've* gone. That he hasn't called me yet to find out is something I start to contemplate as I lower the radio to a dull boom and refocus on the road. The wide expanse of the motorway that's no longer dark.

The frosty winter night lit up by flashing blue.

Twenty

BHODI

It's been a long time since I last contemplated this much blood.

Iron-y red seeps into my shoes where I'm squatting on the frosty tarmac, my hands wedged to the neck of the man half thrown from the mangled SUV. He's conscious enough to batter my eardrums with his screaming, so he'll probably live, but as the frigid cold seeps into me, threatening the unnatural energy of a real emergency, it's my only comfort.

You see, there's a reason I'm not an A&E nurse and it has nothing to do with avoiding my disarming ex.

"Scoot up." A firefighter drops down beside me. "I've got this one if you can give the other rig a hand? And get some high-vis on. Don't want you getting mowed down too."

That's what happened, apparently. Someone jay-walked across the motorway and caused a pile-up with the four vehicles on the road at this time of night. The bad fortune is biblical, but I'm not the one hanging out of a car window, or unconscious in my lorry cab, or the victim of any of the other incidents that have stretched the ambulance service so thin tonight, so I count my blessings as I move through the scene to the next patient.

By chance, I come across the same firefighter from the major incident a few weeks ago.

He's as tired as I feel. "Merry Christmas," he grunts. "This one's dead."

Blunt, but he's right, and I blow out a stressed breath. I was already late home because someone died before I left the hospital. This is not how tonight was supposed to go.

How was it supposed to go then?

Now there's a question, and I no longer know the answer. When I left the house—the annex—I was happy enough to put one foot in front of the other. Then Tam's texts started rolling in and everything felt lighter.

I'd really love to see you.

Vicious wind whips through the accident scene, but even without the coat I've left hanging in Tam's house, this time, with him on my mind, I don't feel it. Because hope is a powerful thing, and that's what I felt when his messages hit.

I'm not humouring you.

Whatever you're thinking, don't.

"Over here, mate."

The firefighter calls for my help again. I follow him to another smashed-up vehicle, my blood-soaked shoes crunching glass, and it's a while before I look up.

By then, it's near dawn and the air ambulance has arrived.

I'm stood down, and I back away from the scene to sink onto a concrete barrier, the bitter temperature and lack of sleep finally catching up with me, fading adrenaline shuddering through my limbs as it peters out.

There's no warmth in my blood and I need to find my car,

abandoned on the hard shoulder when the police flagged me down and spotted my hospital ID dumped on the dashboard. I need to go *home*, to Tam, but even the thought of him isn't enough to get me moving, and he's probably asleep now anyway.

Or just getting up.

Either way, I need to get to him, but I'm too tired to move. To drive. And so I sit there in the cold and wait for that to change.

"Bhodi!"

I'm leaning hard on my bent knees and it's an effort to raise my head. To turn towards the sound of my own name. It starts to rain, fat drops hitting the ice at my bloodied feet. My chest. My face. I can barely see and I raise my hand to fix that feeling as if I've dropped a couple of benzos.

More than a couple—there's no way what I'm left with as my vision clears is anything close to reality.

It can't be.

Because that would mean the tall figure vaulting barriers and running towards me in the rain is Tam—that he's here—and as much as I don't share the misfortune of the poor souls I've seen tonight, I've never been that lucky.

Twenty-One

BHODI

Luck can change.

It's a singular thought as Tam runs through the rain and sweeps into my current universe, isolated by the disbelief still holding firm.

"*Bhodi.*" He goes to touch me, then thinks better of it at the last second. "What the fuck happened?"

I lack the words to explain it, but I'm not so far gone that I don't realise what Tam's staring at. Me, soaking wet and covered in blood at the side of the road, the fading chaos of a major accident unfolding behind me. *Blood makes him sick.* "Pile-up."

"Can fucking see that." His hands hover again, like he's fighting the urge to check every inch of me for injuries. "Are you hurt?"

I stand to reassure him before he gets blood on him too. "I'm not hurt. I wasn't in the accident—I didn't even see it. Just got roped into the aftermath."

Tam's as wet as me and his dark eyes are a little wild. It takes him a second to process what I'm saying. His gaze bounces between me and the HEMS chopper preparing to take off and he shakes his head a little. "I thought you were dead."

"What?"

"You didn't come home—you didn't answer your phone. Then I drove up on this—" He shudders. "Fuck it. Doesn't matter. Are you okay?"

It does matter—*he* matters. But as I go to tell him so, I sway on my feet and his strong arms are an instant cage around me, taking my weight and hauling me to his chest.

I sink into his embrace without a second thought. Forgetting about my wet clothes and the blood. I bury my face and breathe him in, the horrors of the last few hours tightening their grip, and for however long he holds me in the rain, his warm cinnamon scent is the only thing tethering me to the world.

Tam rubs my back, saying nothing and everything with his potent touch. With his stoicism as the blood of a stranger soaks his clothes too.

I take a deep breath and ease back. "Did you smoke?"

He screws his face up. "Little bit. I was really fucking worried."

"I'm sorry."

"Don't be." He kisses the tip of my nose. "Not being dead is enough."

I nod, slowly, everything we need to say to each other swirling between us in a depthless cloud. "I need to go home."

"You can leave?"

"Yeah."

"Where's your car?"

"I don't know."

"Come on. Let's find it and get your stuff."

How I put one foot in front of the other, I have no idea, but the next thing I know I've abandoned my car in a lay-by, and I'm in the passenger seat of Tam's van, clutching my phone as Fairytale of New York blares from the cantankerous stereo.

"Fucking thing." Tam thumps it, and the impact sends a cigarette box sliding from the dashboard into my lap.

"These yours?"

"No."

"Are you lying?"

"Oui-oui, but I only smoked one."

"I'm not judging you." I shake a cigarette free and wedge it between my lips.

Tam eyes me as he manoeuvres the van out of the ditch where he dumped it and presses the in-vehicle lighter. "You don't smoke."

"Neither do you." I light the cigarette and take the deepest inhale I can find, closing my eyes for a beat. Then I ash it and toss it out the window.

Tam makes no comment. He just drives and I'm grateful. That he showed up, that he's with me. No one's ever done that before, and as storm clouds open above us, I realise that even if he's not on the same page my heart has flipped to when I wasn't paying attention, I still need him to know what he means to me.

I take a breath.

He speaks first. "I love you."

"What?"

Tam steers the van down a dark road—I have no idea what

route he's taking home. "I love you. I'm sorry I didn't tell you the other night. I should have."

"I—what?"

Tam turns his head, slowing the van. "I don't want to freak you out, but this *just sex* bullshit isn't working for me anymore. I fucking love you and I need you to know it. Life's too short to keep that shit in."

I have nothing.

The road reclaims Tam's attention and we drive in silence until I realise we're home.

He exits the van.

I sit, feeling slightly unhinged. He loves me? Even in the best-case scenarios I'd imagined at work tonight, those words never left his mouth.

He loves me?

Nope.

Can't see it.

Because I love him too, and that would mean everything's perfect, and that never happens. Not to me.

The passenger door rips open. Tam offers me his good hand. He links our fingers together and tugs me out of the van. I come upright to his beautiful face and he's not laughing at me. This isn't a joke. "Come inside," he whispers. "I need you clean and warm—I need you *safe*—before I can think straight."

By inside, he means his house. I leave my ruined shoes in the rain, and he shuts the door behind us, flicking a switch as Rudy yawns from his cosy bed, not bothering to navigate the dark to come to us.

Nothing happens.

"Power's still out." Tam opens a kitchen drawer and dumps

tea-lights onto the counter while I stare like a stoned hamster. In another cupboard, he reveals a stash of Mr Kipling pie trays and sets the little candles in them, lighting them with a single match from a battered book.

It's the cutest thing I've ever seen.

And his face in the flickering light?

I can't.

Overcome, I back away, colliding with the doorframe.

Tam flashes to my side. "There's hot water left in the tank. You okay if we shower together?"

"Yeah."

"Sure? I can chuck a bucket of water over my head in the garden—"

I kiss him. Just once, and just enough to remind myself he's real. That he's the solid flesh and bone who cared that I didn't come home and came looking for me. That he says he loves me, and I think he might mean it. "Don't leave."

"I won't. Come on."

He leads me upstairs and helps me out of my wet clothes.

I return the favour and we stare at each other in the glow of the candles he brought with us. "You love me?"

Tam frowns. "It kills me that you find it so hard to believe."

"I—"

"Bhodi, it's okay. Let's get warm, all right? Everything else can wait."

He twists the shower dial and steam fills the room as delayed shock works its way through my system. I'm a critical care nurse. I've seen my fair share of horrific things. But I'm human too, and I'm not as jaded as I used be. What I saw tonight, it hurts, and I know it's not going anywhere for a while.

Tam knows it too. I feel it in the quiet way he eases me

under the hot spray and washes blood and grime from my skin while somehow keeping his cast dry. In the intensity of his stare as he watches me shiver. "We don't have long." The water is already cooling as he nuzzles my cheek. "Tell me what you need."

I think about it for less than a second. "I just need you."

Twenty-Two

TAM

The water cools fast, but I'm faster.

I get Bhodi out of the shower, dry him with a towel, and take him to my room.

To my bed.

Because I know what he means when he says he needs me, and that he trusts me enough to give it to him is the greatest gift in the fucking world.

It makes it easier to handle the subtle tremble still simmering beneath his skin. That he's shaking for a reason that might give him nightmares. Bhodi doesn't deserve bad dreams. He deserves to smile and laugh, and to believe the love I've felt for him over the past few weeks is real.

I leave the towels on the floor and drop my face to Bhodi's neck, breathing him in. He tilts his head, giving me better access, and I weave my hand into his thick, damp hair.

God, he smells good. He always has, and it has nothing to do with outside elements or the soap I washed him with in the shower. It's *him*, and a primal need to claim him for myself, once and for all, washes over me.

River always said I was wolfish. That one day, I'd find my person and basically piss on them. This isn't quite that, but I get the sentiment. I *feel* it, and I sink my teeth into the juncture of Bhodi's throat as candlelight flickers around us.

Bhodi's tough. He doesn't flinch away from the pain. If anything, he leans into it, and I bite harder, embedding a mark that I ghost with the barest brush of my lips, teasing him as a frustrated whoosh of air leaves his lungs.

"Tam, I need you to kiss me."

His voice scrapes over the plea, compelling me to comply, as if I could ever refuse him. I bring our mouths together, slipping my tongue between his lips, owning him with it, *giving* myself to it as my head spins with the heat of it.

Sensual and raw, it's every shade of perfect, and I can't get enough. I can't breathe and I don't want to. Not if it means stopping this for the sake of a little oxygen.

Nice sentiment, but I'm human. The tightness in my lungs gets the better of me, and I pull back, getting my reward in his wide eyes and flushed face. In the slow smirk that's starting to chip away at the trauma he's brought home.

I love you.

With that on my mind as I kiss him again, I push him onto the bed, feeling him already hard against my leg, while I've been a rod of pent-up arousal since we stepped into the shower. My dick *aches*—I need this as much as he does. I need *him* and he knows it, sitting up to reach for me.

"No," I whisper. "Let me love you. Please?"

Bhodi hesitates, but he must see in my face that I can't be moved, and after a beat, he nods and lies back on the bed.

I crawl over him, spreading his legs, a low rumble of a groan rolling through me as I kiss his thigh, scraping my scruffy jaw over his sensitive skin.

Bhodi grits out a curse, squirming.

I laugh and pin him down, repeating the motion over and over until his spine arches from the bed and I'll die if I don't get his cock in my mouth.

With no warning, I swallow him whole, and Bhodi swears louder this time, his hands in my hair, his strong thighs a vice around my head, as consuming as he is when he's fucking me.

It's not the first time I've blown him, and God willing, it won't be the last. But this feels different. Timeless, and yet somehow brand-new. I can't get enough—and *that's* not new. Not even close. But long minutes pass before I come up for air with salt on my tongue.

Bhodi stares down at me. "You're playing roulette with my stamina if you want me to fuck you."

I always want him to fuck me. He's amazing at it. But it's not on my mind right now. I move up the bed until I'm looming over him, keeping my weight to myself as he ignores his own warning and surges up to take my mouth, his soft lips as harsh and demanding as they'll ever be, breaking my resolve to tease him a little, to draw this out, my imagination writing cheques my willpower can't cash. "I was hoping you'd let me fuck *you*."

Bhodi blinks, his jewel-bright eyes already dark with desire. "Let you?"

"I'm not a bloke who makes assumptions."

He snorts. "There's no scenario where me wanting you to fuck me isn't a given. Only being inside *you* comes close."

"Now, you say that..." I'm still hovering over him, my dick screaming out for friction. "What if I'm shit at it?"

Bhodi starts to laugh. Then changes his mind and knocks my elbows, bringing me crashing down on him as he seizes my jaw in his hot hand. "Nothing between us could ever be bad."

"I'm not always okay."

Humour dies, obliterated by deeper emotion as we stare at each other in the dim glow of the room. Bhodi strokes my cheekbone with the pad of his thumb. "Neither am I."

"I love you."

His eyes redden. "I love you too—I'm so fucking sorry it scares me so much."

I take his hand, kissing his wrist before I bring it to the pillow above his head. "Don't ever be sorry for loving me. I *know* how lucky I am that you found me."

Doubt looms in his gaze. I need to vanquish it, but I know I can't. Not in one night. This thing between us—this love, this bond. It needs time, and I'm here for it.

I kiss the worries from Bhodi's lips and we roll around on the bed for what feels like hours. A lifetime. Until I'm a mindless mess for anything but him. For the want in his eyes, and flush creeping up his perfect pale torso. For the dig of his fingers into my back as he urges me to press inside him.

The feel of him tight around me is deliriously fucking good. I slide forward, slow at first—*careful*. But a cautious fuck isn't the kind of care Bhodi needs right now and another carnal rumble rolls through me, my body craving more as much as he is, the slick, blunt head of my cock driving deeper.

Bhodi groans, hips chasing friction. Chasing heat. Leaning into the stretch and burn I know so well. "Harder."

I fuck him harder. Not faster. Punching my pelvis forward, searching for the spot that will make him forget everything—what he saw at the scene of that accident, that it's two days before Christmas. His own fucking name by the time I'm done with him.

But this is more than fucking. I'm buried in Bhodi's body like it's my home. Like it's the safest place I've ever been and I'm never going to leave. And like everything else, it should scare *me*. But it doesn't. I'm not afraid to love Bhodi. I never have been. It just took me a while to figure it out, and the thought makes me smile as a wave of bliss unhinges my jaw and I press my forehead to Bhodi's, my breath matching his in short, sharp gasps.

We're close, in every sense of the word. I'm fucking him so slowly that his eyes roll with every thrust, but it has nothing on the effect it's having on me. My heart thumps with a blazing tattoo, pleasure gripping every nerve and muscle in my scarred body. My blood *burns* as it pumps through my veins at breakneck speed, and my soul?

Bhodi's.

Forever and a day.

Or at least for as long as he'll have me.

I don't have the words to express that to him right now. I can only fuck him, sinking my gaze into him as his heated exhales dance over my skin, and hope he hears every little thing I haven't said yet. The things I need to say *louder*, until they're imprinted on his heart and his battered self-esteem stands up for him.

The snap of my hips grows louder. We shunt along the bed as Bhodi meets me thrust for thrust, and we become nothing but the crazed sensation binding us together.

Bhodi's dick weeps against his stomach. I grip it in my fist, feverish, insatiable need sweeping over me, and my world narrows to the sweet bliss that's going to ruin me.

He comes. Like, *really* fucking comes, his whole body jerking from the force of it, a rough, punched-out groan ripping from his chest. He's so beautiful, I'm lost. But then that wave of sweet destruction finds me, and I detonate too, every sinew straining with release, euphoria echoing in my head until I'm nothing but how it feels to dive into his awed gaze and stay there for the rest of my fucking life.

Instead, maybe I fall asleep.

Or maybe he does.

All I know is that I'm dazed as fuck and him calling my name feels like a distant dream until I dial back into the universe.

I refocus.

Bhodi kisses me, biting my lips. "Fuck me again? Please?"

I fuck him all day.

Twenty-Three

BHODI

I wake up with no clue who I am, where I am, or how I got there.

It's dark, but fading. Morning, maybe. I'm not sure. All I know for certain is that I'm not in my bed. That I'm in Tam's bed, in his house, and he's right here next to me.

I touch him to be sure, tucking a lock of his wild hair back from his face.

For a long moment of sheer stillness, nothing happens. Then he stirs and his eyes crack open, unfocussed and tired, and he reaches for me with a clumsy hand. "You're okay?"

Of course I am. I'm with him, but he doesn't seem awake enough to hear me whatever I say, so I kiss his cheek and find his hand under the sheets. "I love you. Go back to sleep."

Tam's gone so fast it's hard to believe he was awake at all. I watch him for a while, pondering that it's the first time I've woken before him and the first time we've slept together in his bed after fucking so many times I lost count.

My body aches in all the right ways. I shift, breathing through it, stretching out on my back with our clasped hands resting on my abdomen while Tam sleeps beside me, and it's so perfect I want to go back to sleep so I can wake up to it again. But I can't find the will. I've slept enough. Now it's time to face the day and whatever it brings.

I need a shower. After hours lost to stroking my fingers through Tam's hair, I force myself up and out of bed before I remember the power cut blanketing the village the last time I was awake.

It's still in force. Tam's cute little Mr Kipling tea-lights have long since died out and nothing else works, leaving me no option but to feed Rudy and let him out before I jump beneath the cold shower spray to wash my skin clean of stale sweat, lube, and other things.

I'm shivering on the landing when the rumble of a vehicle sounds outside.

Wrapped in a towel, I peek out of the landing window.

Sab.

Shit.

I find some clothes and throw them on, dashing downstairs before Rudy can bark up a storm.

He barks anyway, but at least I tried.

I open the front door as Sab vaults the gate.

He spots me and relief floods his tense features. "Thank fuck for that. I thought you'd both carked it."

"What?"

"Tam's phone's off, and the last time I spoke to him, he thought you were dead."

"Last night?"

"No, the night before."

I've lost track of my days. I can't remember when we came back here. Whether it was morning or night. I can't remember anything except Tam telling me he loves me in every way possible, and I'm okay with that. More than okay.

I'm not okay with the worry lining Sab's face.

I step back, waving him inside. It takes him seconds to find Tam's abandoned phone and figure out the power situation. A little longer to jog upstairs and return with a smirk on his face.

"You wore him out."

"He tell you that?"

"Not with words. I can tell by looking at him that he's wrecked."

Guilt threatens the glow I woke up with.

Sab steps closer. "Don't get in your feelings about it. This happens sometimes when that big grumpy heart gets the better of him. He'll be fine when he's slept it off."

I reach for the teabags before I remember nothing works. "How do you know his heart got the better of him?"

"He called me when he didn't know where you were." Sab moves to the log burner and fiddles around with it. "And now you have teeth marks on your neck, so I'm guessing he found you."

My hand flies to my neck and the *deep* hickey Tam left there. "Uh. Yeah. He found me."

Sab snorts and goes back to lighting the fire. It's kind of cosy. Then he rises and his gaze flickers to the stairs again, and I notice his clenched hands and tight shoulders.

"What's the matter?"

"Hmm?"

I slide off the stool I've sunk onto and pad to where Sab

hovers in the middle of Tam's living space, his entire frame a knotted mess of tension. "What's wrong?"

Conflict rages in eyes that are so much like his brother's, but at the same time, a world away from Tam. "I need some money."

"Okay." I'm already searching for the bag I dumped somewhere before Tam steered me upstairs. "I have some cash."

Sab stops me. "Bhodi, I don't need a tenner. I need a lot of money and I need it today."

"You were going to borrow it off Tam?"

"I don't know if he'll have it, but I was going to ask."

"So ask him."

"I can't." Sab scrubs a hand down his face. "I know Tam—how he gets when he's this tired. He's not with it enough to make that kind of decision, and that's not going to change anytime soon."

I absorb that, and guilt does a number on me again. But I'm familiar enough with the progression of acute fatigue to know it's brought on by more than one sleepless night of stress and worry. That Tam's been working every hour under the sun to finish his orders by Christmas.

And that I'm a hundred percent going to help his brother. "How much do you need?"

The power comes back on midafternoon. By then, I'm a few grand lighter and aware it's the day before Christmas Eve.

"I don't know when you'll get it back."

I push Sab out the door. "It doesn't matter. Go get your daughter."

The lights on Tam's Christmas tree glow warm and white. They sway a little in the slight breeze from his ancient windows, casting jumpy little sparks on the walls, and I stare at them for ages. Hours, maybe, until movement upstairs nudges me out of my daze.

I hear footsteps and the whine of the ancient pipes funnelling water around Tam's house.

Then he shuffles downstairs and blinks. "Is this a fucking dream?"

I'm standing by the Christmas tree, wearing his sweats and no shirt, the scent of the only food I could find to cook— chicken and bacon—filtering from the kitchen. "Depends if it's a good dream or not."

Tam steps forward, but he's forced to stop as he winces and rubs his back.

I go to him.

He winds his arms around me, smelling of cinnamon and toothpaste. "Bhodi, any dreams that involve you are the best I've ever had."

I don't realise how much I need to hear that until his words hit me like a wrecking ball, punching the air from my lungs and burning my eyes.

Tam pushes my chin up with his knuckles. "I'm sorry I didn't tell you I loved you sooner. It kills me that you spent even a fucking minute thinking everything between us was anything less than it is."

"I didn't tell you I loved you either." I pull him a little closer and notice the bite mark *I've* left on his collarbone. "I had it in my head it was the last thing you'd want to hear and you'd run a mile."

Honest empathy flares in Tam's dark gaze. "Maybe I would

have in the beginning, but I'd have come back. This..." He presses his palm to his heart and then mine. "...it would've caught up with me eventually. You can't hide from something that burns this bright."

"Say that in French."

He obliges.

I think.

In truth he could be saying anything, but as he breaks off to yawn, I know it doesn't matter. That whatever he's saying, it's the truth, and from Tam, it always will be.

He's still exhausted. I remember what he told me about the fatigue he's sometimes plagued with, and combined with Sab's prophecy, I don't want him on his feet or wasting energy worrying about my self-esteem.

I steer him to the couch and sit him down. I bring him hot food and sweet tea. No cakes, though. He's eaten them all.

Tam inhales everything I put in front of him. Then he dumps his head in my lap and drowses in front of an animated film he calls *L'Enfant au grelot* until I remember the phones I put on charge when the power came back on.

I pass him his and turn mine on. Messages and missed calls light up the screen. Some are from work, but most are Tam, and the concern he had for me heightens with every notification I click through.

Love warms my chest again. I lean down to kiss him.

He kisses me back, then pulls back, tilting his head. "What is it?"

"Nothing." I shake my head. "I'm just not used to someone noticing I'm not home."

"I noticed."

"I know."

We share a moment. Then Tam goes back to his own phone, frowning as he swipes through whatever he's missed while the power was out.

I open a message from my boss, but Tam's rising stress distracts me from taking it in. "What's wrong?"

His frown deepens. "Was Sab here?"

"This morning. He was worried he couldn't get hold of you —oh, and he needed some money to pay a family law specialist. Sorry, it slipped my mind."

Tam starts to get up.

I stay him. "It's okay. I gave it to him and he said he'd call you later."

"You—what?" Tam blinks hard. "You gave him money?"

"Uh. Yeah. He seemed pretty desperate, and I had it in my savings so...wait. You don't think he needed it for—"

Tam shakes his head. "Fuck, no. Even at his worst, he'd never have done that. It's just—fuck. How much was it?"

I name the figure.

Tam's eyes widen. "Shit."

"What?"

"I don't have that much to pay you back."

"You don't need to pay me back. I loaned it to him, not you."

"You loaned it to him *for* me. Because I wasn't there when I should've been."

"You were asleep," I counter. "Because you'd been up for days looking for me, then fucking my brains out. And honestly, I don't care if I never see that money again. What he needed it for is more important than just about anything."

Tam surges upright without warning.

I find myself on my back, his weight pinning me down in an

almost perfect reenactment of how he fucked me last night—yesterday, whenever it was.

He grips my throat and kisses me. "I fucking love you."

"I love you too."

"Yeah?"

I flex my hips, on instinct more than anything else, and I've learned the hard way that how I feel about someone has nothing to do with how horny they make me. But with Tam, everything's different—*I'm* different, and my physical reaction to him means as much as anything I could say.

He feels it too, and it's a while before we come up for air.

I'm naked and sweaty again by the time I remember the work message on my phone.

I read it while Tam lets Rudy out, my mind still half on how well Tam fucks me, and how lucky I am that I got to find my unicorn lover. It takes a second to compute the words on the screen. Then I'm distracted by Tam coming back and my brain reroutes to fucking. Because he's still naked, and so am I. "You know, for someone who doesn't top, you're amazingly good at it."

Tam grins and sinks onto the couch beside me. "I said I bottomed most often, not that I never topped. And you kinda sprang your mad skills on me too. I had a lot to live up to."

I start to scoff, but Tam slaps a hand over my mouth, and he keeps it there until whatever the devil on my shoulder was about to say is gone.

While he's at it, he peers at my phone screen, reading the email from the nurse manager at the hospital. "Does that mean what I think it means?"

"Yup. No work until January."

He nods, frowning like he does sometimes just because his

face falls that way, but I'm still extra enough to read too much into it.

"What? What are you thinking?"

"I'm thinking..." Tam tugs me into his lap, already half hard again. "...that I couldn't love you more, but I'm going to try, *and* that I can't fucking wait to spend Christmas with you."

Epilogue

TAM

One year later...

Turns out I *can* love Bhodi more. I felt it every moment we spent together that Christmas, and every day after.

Could love my brother less, though, now he's living in my fucking annex and giving me shit every spare moment he gets. Thank the Lord life as a single dad doesn't give him much free time, especially since he volunteered to fix the roof of my house in the rain.

Not that being a drowned rat stops Sab getting in my face every two seconds when I have shit to do. *Important* shit—that he knows all about and still won't shut the fuck up.

"Are you doing it today?"

"No."

"Why not?"

"It's raining."

"So?"

"So..." I go to the studio door and go to shut it in his face, kicking his booted foot aside. "It's not gonna rain *tomorrow*, and by then Bhodi will have had some sleep."

"Scared he'll say yes by accident?"

"Fuck off." I shut Sab out and wait for his laughing footsteps to retreat before returning to my desk and the unexploded bomb I've been keeping in the drawer for the last few weeks.

I pull out the small wooden box and open it, revealing the ring I had made by the fire dancer who lives on Firefly Hill. Honestly, I wasn't expecting it to be so fucking perfect, but with the way my life has gone since I met Bhodi, it fits, and I love how the light catches the silver almost as much as I love him. As much as I smile through missing him as I go to bed early knowing he'll be there when I wake up. Most nights he works, I wait up for him, but it's been a long month, and I'm tired. And someone has to be up at the crack of dawn to cook the literal fucking *goose* Sab brought home yesterday and dumped in my fridge.

It's hard to sleep without him, though. Bhodi, not Sab. I've grown used to his life-affirming presence in the bed that's been resolutely ours since Bhodi accepted a permanent position at the hospital. His muscular frame curved around mine, or me curled around him. Like sex, we swap spoons depending on the mood, and I like both.

I like it *all*, and I love him.

It's late when I wake to soft lips at my neck. Or maybe it's early, I can't tell. And it doesn't matter. Nothing does as Bhodi rolls me over, his skin wet from a recent shower, and lowers his tight heat onto my dick.

Merde. If I had to pick a favourite, it would be this: Bhodi dominating me while taking what he wants at the same time. Watching him ride me is every fantasy I never knew I had, and I come so hard and so fast it's almost embarrassing. Except, he comes fast too. And we laugh, and after a quick clean up, I'm asleep again with another smile on my face.

I'm still smiling when I wake up to the most perfect Christmas morning. Stardust Lane lives up to its name and glittery frost stretches as far as I can bring myself to look while Bhodi is in my arms.

I let him sleep for a bit, grateful Sab took Rudy to the annex for the night. They're not exactly friends, but Rudy likes to guard the baby, and Sab isn't sad about it.

"Mornin'."

Bhodi's sleepy voice erases all thoughts of Sab from my mind.

I turn my head and he's right there, those eyes still jewel-bright no matter how tired he is. "Morning. You don't have to be awake yet."

"Maybe I want to be."

"Yeah?"

"Yeah." He kisses my neck with far less heat than he did in the early hours, but with just as much love. "I want to see Esme open her presents."

My heart swells impossibly bigger. Thanks to the money Bhodi lent Sab, and a drug raid on Charmaine's house, Esme lives with Sab full-time with only supervised contact with her mum. It's the best possible outcome, even though my brother is living with a baby in a studio apartment until he can sort something else. And one of *the* best things about it?

I get to see Bhodi and Esme bond on an almost daily basis and I love that so much it hurts.

We get up and Christmas Day unfolds like a fucking fairytale. I cook Sab's goose with minimal heckling from him, while he does everything else and Bhodi plays with the baby.

When present time hits, he gives me a pot of jewel-blue ink to go with the handwritten note he's been working on for a week, and I give him a tea mug with filthy French words inscribed inside. Because we decided last year that loving each other was the best gift we'd ever have. Staring death in the face, whether it's your own or a stranger's, does that to a man, and I'm okay with it as long as I get to keep Bhodi.

At midnight, I kick Sab out. He's so excited he can barely contain himself and Bhodi's starting to notice.

"Did he drink all that brandy your mum sent?"

I spy the half-empty bottle on the counter and swipe it, taking a healthy swig. "No, that was me."

Bhodi laughs. "Fair enough. You want to watch Die Hard in bed?"

"In a minute."

He turns his head from where he's closing the vents on the log burner, the Christmas tree sparkling with the only light left in the room, and he's so beautiful my breath catches, stealing the words I've been practising all day.

"I love you."

Yup. That wasn't it, though it's close.

Bhodi grins and comes to where I'm hovering by the tree. "I love you too. Thanks for an amazing day."

"It was amazing because of you."

"I didn't do anything."

"You exist, and you have no fucking idea how life-changing that's been for me—for Sab and Esme too."

He takes a breath to counter the sentiment, but catches himself, something he's better at these days. Letting me love him without question. "Thanks for saying that. It means a lot."

"There's more."

Curiosity lights his gaze.

"I want to marry you."

That's not how the script goes either, but the surprise in Bhodi's face is worth the brevity. The shock. And then the unfettered joy he can't hide. "*You* want to get married?"

"Oui-oui. To *you*. I got a ring and everything."

Bhodi frowns and I realise I've slipped into French entirely.

I dig in my pocket and find the box. Open it and think about dropping to one knee, but his grip on my arms keeps me on my feet. "All right. Let me say it properly. Will you fucking marry me?"

Bhodi's frown fades like it was never there at all. Happiness expands as I slide the ring made from an antique pen nib onto his finger. Then he sweeps *me* off my feet, spinning me around, and Christmas on Stardust Lane gifts me another day with him that I'll never, ever forget.

Thank you so much for reading Christmas On Stardust Lane! Please don't skip this part! If you want to know more about the Rebel Kings MC series (and Skylar), you can binge the whole series on Kindle Unlimited.

The big firefighter and the dancer from up the hill can be found in Christmas On Firefly Hill.

AND, for anyone who's curious about Sab, yes he WILL be getting his own book. Christmas On Cosmic Avenue will be with us 2025 and I promise to give him the happy ending he deserves. In the meantime, if you're already missing him, **Christmas On Stardust Lane is now out in a special, limited edition hardback with bonus content from Sab's POV.**

Other Holiday Titles

Check them out on my Amazon author page <3

About the Author

Right now, Instagram is the best way to keep up with Garrett. Click on the icon below to follow, or search @garrett_leigh

Bonus Material available for all books on Garrett's Patreon account. Includes short stories from the Rebel Kings (LOADS), Misfits, Slide, Strays, What Remains, Dream, and much more. Sign up here: https://www.patreon.com/garrettleigh

Facebook Fan Group, Garrett's Den.

Garrett is also an award winning cover artist, taking the silver medal at the Benjamin Franklin Book Awards in 2016. She designs for various publishing houses and independent authors at https://www.blackjazzdesign.com

Connect with Garrett
www.garrettleigh.com

Also by Garrett Leigh

Info for all my books can be found on my website: http://www.
garrettleigh.com